BACK COVER

I am the ghost that haunts your dreams. I am a liar, a protector ... a killer... I am death.

You think you know my story, but you have no idea. My death was just the beginning. In the years since I escaped the shadow organization that owned me, my vow to protect my family is the only thing keeping me alive.

Until I meet *her*.

Too bad I need the monster to protect her from the demons of her past.

Too bad she's not *that* innocent.

Cliff-hanger Warning: I know you want the whole story right now. But that's not how things went down. And I think you know by now that when it comes to ORUS, things don't always go according to f*cking plan.

(Deep *is Book 1 of the* 

ll come in Book 2, Deeper)

DEEP

M. MALONE
NANA MALONE

MALONE

ALSO BY M. MALONE & NANA MALONE

- The Shameless Trilogy -

Shameless

Shameful

UnAshamed

- The Force Duet -

Force

Enforce

- The Deep Duet -

Deep

Deeper

A MALONE SQUARED PUBLICATION

Print ISBN: 978-1-946961-14-3

1

"If you're done chatting with your boyfriend, it's showtime."

Rafe pocketed his phone and rolled his eyes at his sometimes partner, Oskar Mueller, from Blake Security.

"What's the matter, sweetheart, you don't want me having anyone else to talk to? It's okay to be jealous, you know. You just have to tell me and you can have all my attention." Rafe blew the German a kiss.

It was sure to piss the guy off, but Oskar's anger was better than his asking questions Rafe wasn't ready to answer. The phone calls that wouldn't stop needed to remain his secret for now.

Oskar bared his teeth and flipped the safety off on his weapon. The two had a slightly contentious relationship, but Rafe was certain the German would come around eventually. Rafe had once tried to kill him, sure, but how long could anyone really stay mad about that?

"Whatever. Let's do this. I don't want this asshole getting away again."

Rafe nodded briskly. No one was getting away on his watch. Oskar headed north and Rafe went east, as they'd planned. The company tech guru, Matthias, had already given them the route Douchebag would be taking.

Douchebag's real name was Nathan Miller. Normally Blake Security would let the cops deal with a drug dealer, but Nathan had an interesting forced-recruitment scenario going on. He also had a history of pulling women into his schemes, women that he abused and kept against their will. *That* ticked off every single member of the team, so Rafe and Oskar had been sent to deliver a cease and desist letter of sorts.

Rafe stepped out from the alley just as Nathan rounded the corner.

Douchebag sneered even though Rafe had a good two inches on him. "Watch where you're walking, asshole."

Rafe cracked his neck even as a shot of adrenaline flooded his veins. He would never admit it out loud, but he fucking lived for this shit. "You know what? I don't think I will."

His first jab sent the guy's head snapping back.

"What the fu—"

Poor Nathan didn't get another word in because he was tasting Rafe's knuckles again. "Now, Nathan... you, me and my associate, if he ever gets here, are going to have a heart-to-heart about your business practices. And the way you treat women."

At his words, a small blond head peeked out from behind Nathan. In one smooth motion, Rafe shoved Nathan to the side and stepped in front of the girl.

"Hi, Callie. Your brother sent us."

Her eyes immediately filled with tears, but she nodded frantically.

"I don't think you know who the fuck you're dealing with," Nathan growled from behind him.

Before Nathan was even done with the sentence, Rafe had his gun in the guy's face. That shut him up pretty quickly.

"Callie, I need you to wait for us beside that Dumpster. And close your eyes. Okay?" He didn't take his eyes off Nathan, but he listened to the soft fall of Callie's footsteps as she obeyed.

Nathan glared at him even as Oskar strolled down the opposing alleyway. When he saw Rafe's gun out, he looked pissed.

"Oh hell, you got started without me?"

"Next time don't bother to pretty yourself up for me.

It's no use really. Your face is your face. And you can relax. I left plenty of ass kicking for you."

Oskar just grinned. "You're so good to me," he said as he unsheathed his knives. As his partner moved forward, Rafe walked to Callie and held out a hand to her. He led her around the corner so she wouldn't have to see what came next.

Callie flinched and peered up at Rafe from tired eyes. Her makeup had run, so there were dark smudges on her cheeks. It was a look he'd seen many times before, the universal expression of defeat. That was what it looked like when good people gave up hope.

"What happens now? Nathan will never let me go."

Rafe wasn't good at this part. The comforting, the drying of the tears. Years ago he had been. He'd been the person who held his baby sister when she cried and told her that everything would be okay. Then he'd had to leave her, and all that emotion ceased to exist.

But this was supposed to be a new beginning, wasn't it? Going forward, he could decide what kind of man he would be.

"He *will* let you go. I'm going to make sure of it." Rafe didn't touch her, wasn't sure if it would frighten her, but he did gesture the other direction to let her know that it was safe to walk that way. They didn't need to stay; Oskar had things well in hand.

As Rafe turned to walk behind her, his skin prickled. He paused, then glanced over his shoulder. Oskar already had Nathan on the ground and was securing him with zip ties. Rafe's eyes scanned over the alley and then up to the roof of the buildings above. It was dark, and only a few of the windows in the building were lit up. Most people were asleep right now, completely unaware of the things happening floors below. People in this neighborhood didn't *want* to be aware of what was happening outside. The less you knew, the safer you were.

Rafe knew all about that.

Nathan was on the ground, no longer struggling. In about an hour, he'd be found by the police with a kilo of cocaine strapped to him and a weapon that had been used in a murder a year ago.

The gun was actually Nathan's; they hadn't manufactured that. He'd wiped it down and asked one of his runners to dispose of it. That same runner had come to Blake Security for help getting his sister away from Nathan.

"All good?" Oskar appeared at his elbow, his eyes narrowing as Rafe continued to peer at the buildings around them.

"Yeah. Just had a feeling..."

Oskar snorted. "Your Spidey sense was tingling?"

Rafe scowled. "You can never be too careful."

"You don't need to be so jumpy. You're not a narc anymore, remember? We're the good guys."

"I was never a narc," Rafe responded automatically. But as they led Callie back to the SUV they'd parked a few streets over, the other man's words rolled around in his mind.

The good guys.

What did that even mean? Fucking guys up in dark alleys, planting evidence? Not so different from his past. Except now he was the one making the decisions.

For years he'd been a member of ORUS, an elite shadow organization supporting the US government. Now he was his own man, no longer a weapon to be used for unknown agendas. He could decide what was right and what was wrong. After what they'd done, Callie would be going home and sleeping in her own bed, safe and sound. The streets of New York would have one less asshole peddling poison to those too vulnerable to protect themselves.

Messy, yes. But it was the best result they could have asked for. Rafe had learned over the years that he couldn't always make things right, but he could try to make them better.

Maybe better was enough. For now.

SHE HAD no idea what he was doing.

Diana Vandergraff squinted and then blinked as if her eyes were deliberately deceiving her. She watched in disbelief as her target walked away from the drug dealer, instead approaching the woman behind him. Even from a distance and through binoculars, she could see that his movements were gentle. Reassuring.

He was reassuring her? Nothing about this made sense.

Then again, nothing about Rafael DeMarco made sense. And she would know. She'd been watching him for ages now.

Stalking. You've been stalking him.

Diana smiled in satisfaction. Yes, she'd been keeping tabs on DeMarco for almost a year. It was fitting, really. The hunter becoming the prey. After all the people DeMarco had tormented, now he was the one who was looking over his shoulder.

At first she'd only tailed him to and from his apartment. Ideally, she'd have loved to get in there and look around right away, but the place was like a fortress. While posing as a pizza delivery girl coming to the wrong door, she'd noticed the steel contacts around the doorframe. Definitely not your average security system. Besides that, DeMarco rarely left the place except to go to a modified warehouse in Manhattan. The building had been demolished and rebuilt in the early 90s. The first five floors were still warehouse spaces, but a commercial building had been constructed on top of that, boasting some twenty floors. And at the very top sat a penthouse... home of Blake Security.

So far she hadn't been able to determine exactly what he did there. Either way, she wouldn't give up until she'd peeled back every layer DeMarco had. It didn't matter how long it took or that she was currently cold, cramped, and uncomfortable while spying on him from a rooftop.

It had been too long, and she'd come too far to give up now.

Movement below caught her eye, and she swung the binoculars toward the blond giant Rafe had met up with earlier.

Oskar Mueller. German. Employed by Blake Security for five years. Master's degrees in finance and economics. Employment history blank for years until he started working for Blake Security.

Her mind ran through all the available data she'd uncovered on Mueller. Information was hard to come by on everyone employed by Blake Security. Something she was sure was deliberate. But she'd been able to find out the basics from a routine background check.

Mueller was currently roughing up the drug dealer and finally dropped him with one punch to the face. Diana winced. Not that she felt any sympathy. The guy was clearly not a Cub Scout leader. Everything she'd uncovered led her to believe the firm had a great reputation.

Which didn't explain why the hell they'd employ a known killer like DeMarco.

Her fingers tightened around the binoculars. Hatred was a powerful drug, and for years she'd been fueled on a steady diet of it for the man who'd killed her father. He was her personal bogeyman and the personification of everything evil in this world. Rafael DeMarco was the very thing that tormented her dreams.

"Deep breaths, Diana. Deep breaths," she whispered to herself, closing her eyes briefly to bring her emotional reaction under control. Emotions weren't something she allowed herself to indulge anymore. They only got in the way. The last person she'd loved, truly loved, had been murdered right in front of her, and she'd been haunted by the loss ever since. There was room in her life now for only one thing, and it wasn't love.

It was vengeance.

Her eyes popped open at the sounds below. Mueller had finished with the now-unconscious man in the alley, and DeMarco was still talking to the woman. Part of her wanted to stand up and scream, warning the other woman.

Don't trust him.

He's not as he appears.

DeMarco had taken away the last person who loved her, and for what? Money? Diana ached at the thought that her father had suffered because he was trying to protect her legacy. The Jewel of the Sea had been the only thing left of her mother, and it had been willed to Diana. No doubt her father had received many offers to buy it after her mother's death, but he'd always told her that he would protect it for her until she grew up.

He'd never had the chance to keep that promise.

Diana adjusted slightly, moving her leg to stop it from cramping. The wind blew a harsh caress against her exposed cheek, and she tugged the black knit cap covering her hair lower. DeMarco was still talking to the woman. What could he be saying that would take this long? But there was no denying the difference in his body language when talking to the woman versus the guy in the alley or Mueller.

Diana smiled as ideas sprang to her mind. For the past year, she'd laid the groundwork to take DeMarco down to the best of her ability, even establishing a fake lease and utilities under an alias. All it had taken was paying the right people at the right times. But none of it meant anything if she couldn't get close to him.

But it appeared that big, bad DeMarco had a weakness.

"So you have a knight-in-shining-armor complex, huh? I can use that."

Just then DeMarco paused and glanced up and over his shoulder. It shouldn't have caused any reaction after all this time, but she thought again how wrong it was that he would be handsome. But wasn't that always the way of things? From this distance, she couldn't make out the expression on his face, but Diana got a quick impression of impatience and suspicion before she ducked down behind the brick barrier of the roof.

There was no way he could have seen her from such a distance, right? Despite all the reports she'd read to the contrary, Rafael DeMarco wasn't superhuman. He was fallible just like all of them. Blood and bone. He would bleed red just like anyone else.

And just like any other man, he couldn't resist a damsel in distress.

Diana stood slowly and then peered over the ledge again. The alley below was empty save for the still body of the drug dealer. She needed to get out of here. Even in this neighborhood, a body drew heat. Attention she couldn't afford right now.

After all, she had a plan to execute. She smiled to herself before gathering her equipment.

"One damsel, coming right up."

2

Diana watched Rafe from across the street.

There he was with his friends. His stride was easy, as if he didn't have any cares in the world. What was that like?

Her whole life, she'd always felt *uncomfortable*. Like she was waiting for something bad to happen. *Thank you, Rafael DeMarco*. Hell yeah, it was his fault. The day he'd come into her life, she'd been scarred in ways she could never have predicted.

With her long-lens camera, she took several photos, zooming in on the digital images as they came up. The tall one with the cocky stride, he was Noah Blake. Blake Security was his.

Had he been the one to call the hit on her father? Was Rafe *just* a hired assassin? There were so many questions there. Before a few years ago, Noah Blake hadn't seemed to exist beyond a social security number and patchy school records. Not so much as a menial job at a 7-Eleven.

And then suddenly there he was with enough money to open his own business. A *very* nice business considering Blake Security occupied the penthouse of this building. She took more photos. Snap, snap, snap, snap. The soft click of the shutter filled the silence in the car.

Blake had his arm wrapped around a woman with a baby strapped to her. Her long, curly hair was flowing in the wind behind her. The way he tucked his arm around her and held her protectively made it clear they were together. A family unit. No one was breaking them apart.

The one she didn't know was the younger guy. Oh, he was just as tall and looked just about as deadly as Noah and Rafe did. Dark hair, some tattoos peeking out from under his T-shirt. Of all the guys, he was the hardest to pin down. He hardly ever left the building.

She'd managed to catch him skulking out like he didn't want to be seen about a month ago. But that had been it.

She knew from her surveillance over the past several months that there were at least four more. Mueller, the Viking from the other night, and a couple of younger-looking ones. They both had dark hair and more boy-next-door kind of looks.

That left the one who didn't fit. Jonas Castillo. He dressed better than the others, including shoes she recognized as something her brothers would wear. Sometimes a vest, sometimes a suit. Her files said ex-cop. But seriously, what kind of cop dressed like that? He, unlike every other person who worked at Blake, actually had a traceable path. Though a sketchy one. Rumor was Castillo had been sleeping with the wife of the disgraced ex-mayor.

Well lo and behold, the guy ended up dead after putting his wife in the hospital. All fingers pointed at Castillo. But he'd had an airtight alibi complete with video evidence for the hours surrounding the mayor's death. They couldn't make anything stick to him, but he'd been forced out of the department. Within a week, he'd had a job at Blake Security.

She needed to know more. And until she could get in and meet them, the other players on the board would remain question marks. That was okay—she was getting close. At least she hoped she was getting close, because she sure as hell was getting tired.

As she watched Rafe's strides eat up the pavement, the tingle in her belly intensified. What the hell was wrong with her? *Danger, bitch. Danger*. This thing with her libido was getting out of hand. There was something about his swagger that was ultimately appealing. Hell, she was a woman after all.

But that gnawing, longing pull of attraction had only gotten worse. Something at the base level of her nature found him fascinating. Which was a hell of a problem, because how was she going to get her revenge when her body kept thinking about ways to get under him? Okay, on top of him too. She did like to be thorough.

The Bluetooth in her car rang, and she pressed the Yes button. "Hey, Charisse."

"Hey, Di. What are you up to?"

"Oh, you know. A little of this. A little of that."

"Still following Rafe, huh?"

She sighed. "So what if I am?"

"Are you at least being safe?"

"Yes. I'm being safe. I promise. Besides, I already have a plan to get at him."

She could hear her best friend muttering something about saints preserving her. "Shit. Di, do I even want to know how you plan to *get at him*?"

"Probably not. You wouldn't like it." Charisse was her oldest friend from university. She was also the only one who had the whole picture on what she was doing.

She'd given Diana a place to stay while she planned

and a shoulder to cry on when shit got so hard she didn't think she'd be able to continue.

"Di, look, I get it. This guy killed your father, but that's all the more reason you should let the authorities handle it. Because he is a killer and he could hurt you."

"Well, he's going to have a hell of a time. I've been planning for this, training for this. I have given up any semblance of a life just to get this close."

She'd started looking for him three years ago, as soon as she graduated university. She'd dug up her father's old files that she could access, tried to think of anyone who might have information.

She'd been so deadly serious about pursuing him she'd even asked her brothers for help in finding information. They didn't think that a woman was capable of much, so they'd laughed her off. But not before giving her the name of someone who could do the legwork. It had taken time. But she'd been given a name. And a name had been all she needed.

After that, she tracked him. Rafael DeMarco. Italian. Grew up in Connecticut but then moved to Brooklyn. He had a younger sister, Lucia DeMarco, married to Noah Blake with one child.

Rafael DeMarco had never been married as far as she could tell, unlike Noah Blake. *He* was supposed to be dead. He looked pretty damn good for a corpse. If that guy was a vampire, she suddenly saw the appeal of all those sparkly undead.

The first time she'd seen Rafe's obituary, the despair had been deep. She'd been sure she'd lost her only chance to find out why her father had been murdered. But she'd gotten lucky.

She'd had eyes on his sister because she figured Lucia might know something about the people her brother worked for. Then one day out of the blue, Rafe had just walked into Lucia's office. She'd been studying him ever since, getting ready to spring a trap. Hell, it had taken patience and dedication and help. At least she had the funds to finance the help. She couldn't watch him all the time. *Nor should you. Lest you become obsessed.*

"Look, Char, I know you're worried about me, and I appreciate it. But this man is a killer. He took my father away from me. He has to pay."

"I hear that, but you need to be careful. You don't have enough information about him. You say he's a killer. What if he finds out who you are? What if he finds out that you are lying to him? I mean, he killed your father. So he has no qualms about killing innocent people. Maybe he had business with your father, maybe he didn't, but you don't know that he won't hurt you. You're lucky to have what you have. Maybe it's time to move on."

"Charisse, I wish I could explain, but I cannot move on with my life. It feels like I'm stuck in the memory of that day. My father, he wasn't always around, but I know he loved me. And that man took him from me. I can't just let that sit. It's like I'm stuck. I can't move forward."

"I understand. I do. I just— I think what you're doing is dangerous, and I worry about you."

"I appreciate it. But look, right now I'm hidden. No one can see me. No one knows I'm observing them. I'm at his job. I know he goes there every day. I've been tracking his movements. His employer of record is Blake Security. These are things I know. I know he has a sister. She's married to the boss. If I can get a little leverage, then I can guarantee he won't hurt me."

The baby in the carrier strapped to Lucia DeMarco waved a fist and then giggled. Diana couldn't exactly hear it, but she could imagine the sound. And despite herself, a smile tugged at her lips. Lucia DeMarco looked happy. With her handsome husband, smiling at him, walking with friends. Did she know her brother was a killer? Did Noah Blake know what Rafe was capable of?

They look like a family. The pang sliced through her, deep and strong, debilitating enough to make her suck in a short breath. *One day. One day you'll have that.*

Yeah, just as soon as she'd dealt with Rafael DeMarco.

She snapped another picture of the guy she didn't know and then frowned when she zoomed in on the image. He had dots, a series of them on the back of his neck. Just like Rafe did.

What the hell?

She photographed Rafe as usual. She photographed Lucia, but no such dots. But Noah Blake had them too.

What in the ever-loving hell?

"Hello, earth to Diana."

"Sorry, I just—"

"Diana, you said you were following Rafe. Where exactly are you?"

Diana sank in the seat of her car as if Charisse could see her. "Well, about that—"

"Where are you?" Her bestie was not to be fooled.

"I'm across the street from Blake Security."

"Oh my God, are you insane?"

"Relax. It's fine. They can't see me."

"They could have cameras."

"Maybe. But (a) I'm wearing a wig, (b) I'm a tourist taking photos, (c) I keep changing out my rental cars so they don't notice. I'm fine. I got this handled."

"I sure hope you know what you're doing."

So did Diana. Because if she didn't, she might end up dead.

Like your father.

DIANA STARTED down over the edge of the ravine and swallowed hard as saliva filled her mouth. She hated heights. Heights meant she could fall to her death. But hey, details, right? Besides, the whole plan was for it to *look* like she'd nearly tumbled to her death. It was times like this that she needed a rational friend to tell her that her plan was crazy. *Note to self, make more rational friends.* Or hell, any friends. Funny how there wasn't time for friends when you had revenge on the brain.

Ovary up, bitch. This is the plan.

If she wanted her plan to work, it was going to require sacrifice, which meant getting this car down the fucking ravine and then climbing down herself. Time to put on her big-girl thong.

She gathered up her long blond hair and secured it with a ponytail holder. Time to get to work. She only had a couple of hours. She'd been following Rafe DeMarco every Tuesday for months. This was the path he'd take. It was too late for another plan. Besides she's been setting this up for months.

She had selected the perfect spot for this. Right before the guardrail began. As an added bonus, there was a path she could use to initially climb down and a rock outcropping she could stand on to wait for him.

She'd scattered broken glass to make it look like an accident. Once the car was in neutral, she jogged around to the trunk and started to push.

Her ribs throbbed. That asshole in krav maga class had forgotten they were training and had gotten in a brutal hit. She'd have bruises for days. But it wasn't like she could wait to heal up.

Even as the sweat popped on her brow and her body screamed, inch by inch she pushed until she finally started to get some momentum. And then managed to get the car right up to the edge. With one more deep breath, she rolled the car over the edge.

The crash, boom, thud sounds echoed all through the ravine as the car tumbled front-over-end down the jagged edges of rocks. A quick glance at her watch told her she needed to haul ass. DeMarco was likely turning on to the road by now, so she didn't have time to waste.

It was a stupid thing, but she felt a pang of hurt looking at the shiny blue paint she'd picked out, all crumpled and cracked. That was the first car she'd ever bought for herself.

She'd never had her own car before. Her father had preferred for her to be chauffeured, and her brothers had felt the same way. So she'd been excited to pick out a car on her own. And look at it now... a martyr for the cause.

"Your sacrifice will not be for nothing, young Toyota."

The back of the car was now completely smashed and bent, so it looked like the car had skidded off the road and plunged down the embankment. She shivered. Under her coat, she only wore a thin dress, one that clung to her curves. But it was part of the plan, so she'd pushed past the mortification. It would all be worth it soon.

She clasped her forehead, rubbing at the stress ball of tension that had settled behind her eyes. *Now or never.*

The entire scene had been meticulously planned. With a deep breath, she scooted around the guardrail and held her breath as she started down the nearly nonexistent trail. Sand and razor-sharp rocks were more than happy to mingle with her toes and cut up her feet, but she kept moving.

The son of a bitch had better take the bait. *He will.* This whole plan banked on Rafe DeMarco being a decent enough human being to care about someone else potentially being hurt. Either that or curious enough to stop and see what the hell was going on.

The glass was hard to ignore. She just prayed some other stray motorist didn't decide to be a Good Samaritan. But this was an access road, rarely ever traveled.

She shoved aside the lingering feelings of doubt and concern and guilt. This man had taken everything away from her, deliberately and systematically. She was going to return the favor. And she was going to get her life back. It didn't matter how long it took.

She shivered again when she remembered his dark eyes peering at her from behind the mask. He'd just killed her father. Two bullets in the skull. Cold. Efficient. His lips had been set in a firm, grim line.

She'd gasped from her hiding place, the fear and the shock and despair leaking through her body like a chemical spill. She still remembered the sound of his voice as he muttered a single word. "Fuck." When he'd pulled aside the curtain, she'd been so sure he was going to kill her too. Positive he was going to murder her like he'd done her father. But he hadn't. He'd let her live.

That was his first mistake.

Maybe he'd assumed she'd be so traumatized by the situation that she wouldn't remember. Maybe he thought she'd be grateful he hadn't killed her. Maybe he thought she'd forget his face, his voice, the way he made her feel.

Bad luck for him. She remembered that day in startling clarity. The day he'd turned her family upside down. Come to think of it, she needed to have a slogan for when she saw him again. Like in *The Princess Bride.*

"My name is Diana Vandergraff. You killed my father. Prepare to die." She wasn't the villain here, so she wasn't going to have some long, drawn-out bragging speech. But he would know. She'd make sure he understood the series of events that had led to his world crumbling.

She *wanted* him to know.

Before she got her revenge, she'd get the answers she'd been searching for her whole life. Her father hadn't been particularly affectionate or demonstrative, but he'd always been gentle with her. She couldn't imagine any reason that he would be murdered other than for his money. Even as sheltered as she'd been, Diana had seen how people treated them all because of their wealth.

There were quite a few men who had approached her brothers about her simply because she'd inherited such a large trust fund. Men whom she'd had only brief conversations with were suddenly ardent admirers once they found out she was the Vandergraff heiress.

Well, she was an heiress no more. Hell, she didn't even recognize that version of herself, the one who represented her family at society functions, wearing a ball gown and an insipid smile.

That girl was soft. That girl was vulnerable. The moment Diana was out of school, the only identity she knew was avenging angel.

Diana rubbed her hands up and down her arms when she reached the outcropping. The man she was targeting was a killer and a criminal. He had this coming. To do what she had to do, she couldn't be Diana Vandergraff. She needed to be Diana Renquist.

3

"It seems our old friends at Interpol want you back."

Rafe lounged against the far wall of the intake room. He would think after all this time he would be used to rooms with no windows. "What can I tell you, Alan? I'm a likable guy. But no thanks. I like being a civilian. You know, drinking pumpkin ass-tasting lattes or whatever at Starbucks."

His handler didn't seem impressed with his jokes. "Can you be serious for a moment?"

Rafe forced his shoulders to relax. Normally everyone was telling him to loosen up. He used to be a company man, followed the rules to the letter. *But hello, disenchantment, my old friend.*

He didn't miss this. The secrecy, the hiding out. He still checked in every week like clockwork out of habit.

Because there were active cases he had worked on for years. And even though he was a Blake Security man now, he wanted to see those cases play out. Thankfully that was coming to an end.

He'd given his family up for the job. Well, no more. He was done doing favors. He had Lulu back now. He wasn't getting dragged back into some undercover gig.

Right about now, he was in the zero-fucks-to-give category. Besides, it would be next to impossible to make undercover work for him. And he wasn't leaving Lulu vulnerable again. It had been an overly interesting year already. It wasn't like Noah wasn't strong enough or deadly enough to protect his sister. But they'd just gotten their lives started, and he didn't want to bring trouble to their door. Not that trouble didn't seem to find them.

Or at least that was how he rationalized it. "You've got my full attention."

"Glad to hear it. Right now we've got problems from an old friend of yours."

His inner killer, the part of himself he kept chained up in the dungeon of his brain, started to stretch out. *Easy. We don't do that anymore.*

"What now?" He rolled onto the balls of his feet. Ready, poised for action. And that was the underlying problem. He was *always* ready. *Always* poised for action.

Truth be told, he wasn't sure he could *do* normal. What kind of woman wanted a guy who was always ready for a fight... or worse? He knew from his sister's experience that the kind of physical security required for a relationship with someone like him was stifling.

"Do you remember the Vandergraffs?"

Oh hell. Did he ever remember them. As much as he tried to forget, there was no shoving them out of his mind. *Those dark eyes looking up at him.* "Yes, of course I remember them."

Dieter Vandergraff had been a sanctioned hit. The CIA had farmed out the job to ORUS. It had been part of a joint task force effort to see which organization could get the closest. Of course, his former employer had been the one to get it done. *He'd* been the one to get it done.

"What about them?"

There was a knock at the door and Alan called out, "Come in."

"Alan, sorry I'm late." She turned her attention to Rafe. "Agent DeMarco? Long time no see."

Oh shit. Emilie. How long had it been since he'd seen her?

The woman standing on the other side of the room had long hair in such a deep red color that he'd always doubted it could be real. She was pale and statuesque, with the kind of curvy figure and impossibly small waist that usually had men's tongues hanging out. Her eyes were dark, and she blinked at him from behind delicate, fluttery lashes. She was beautiful. Rafe acknowledged the fact in a distant fashion, but when their eyes met, he felt nothing but wariness.

Emilie Durand was the type of woman who could cut your throat and have you smiling throughout the entire thing. *Dangerous.*

"Rafe, you remember Interpol Agent Emilie Durand?"

There was nothing in Alan's voice to indicate hostility, but Rafe got the distinct impression that his handler wasn't too fond of the woman in question. And he understood why.

"Agent Durand."

"Nice to see you again, Agent DeMarco." Emilie held out her hand, and Rafe shook it quickly, pulling back when she held on a moment too long. *Ah, that is going to be a problem*, he thought when he registered the look of interest in her eyes. She wasn't even bothering to hide the fact that she was ogling him. Some things never change.

"Can you bring me up to speed?" He directed the question at Alan, but Agent Durand was the one who answered.

"Since Dieter Vandergraff's death, the family has mostly been quiet. Small-time gigs. We primarily allowed the Austrian authorities to deal with them in whatever manner they saw fit. But it looks like they've gotten into bed with the Russian mob. And they've ramped up their father's old business pursuits and have started making a nuisance of themselves in a major way."

Rafe scowled as he thought of Dieter Vandergraff's sons. At the time he'd taken out their father, they'd been younger, small-time thugs. They certainly hadn't been strong enough or powerful enough to take over their father's empire. Their organization should have withered away, but they'd apparently proved more resilient than he'd thought.

"What do you want from me?" He prayed the answer would be nothing. It was the only job that still haunted him after all these years. *Those dark eyes.*

He'd left one crucial fact off his original report. Dieter's daughter. Their intel had said she wasn't supposed to be at the house. Before she'd had a chance to scream, he had his hand over her mouth. He knew what was in the ORUS playbook for such events. And he knew that as an FBI agent on a joint task force team with the CIA and Interpol, he should have put her in the report. But he hadn't.

His omission might be coming back to bite him in the ass now.

He had taken her to a closet and told her to stay quiet. And she'd been so terrified she did exactly as he asked. He wasn't sure why he'd left her off the report. The Feds and Interpol would've hardly expected him to harm a civilian.

The CIA was a different game. They were almost as brutal as ORUS. So he'd stayed silent about her presence there.

"Interpol has issued a red notice for the Vandergraffs. They're implicated in a massive human trafficking operation that covers most of Western Europe. Of course, they've been on several countries' radar for decades now, as I'm sure you're aware, but they were always very careful to keep their tracks clear."

Rafe ignored the look she sent his way when she said *as I'm sure you're aware* since she'd obviously seen the files relating to their previous operation in Austria. Having been deep undercover with ORUS at the time, his files at the FBI wouldn't have revealed that he was the one responsible for the hit on Dieter Vandergraff, but he figured she could guess. She seemed like the type to read between the lines. Exactly what he didn't need.

"So they're here. In New York?"

"Yes, so we all need to be on alert. Likely they're not

here for vacation. They want something." Alan finally pushed away from the wall and walked closer. Although he'd included them both when he spoke, Rafe was pretty certain the message was for him.

"You think they know we're working on a case against them?"

Alan nodded. "No doubt they're building up their contacts here in North America because they're on the radar of law enforcement agencies in so many countries in Europe. With their contacts, they could easily take up new identities in the States and start an entirely new criminal enterprise here. They just need funds and to partner with the right organization. They appear to be having financial problems."

That took Rafe by surprise. The Vandergraffs had always been a different level of wealthy. He whistled. He couldn't imagine blowing through that kind of money in ten lifetimes. "What do you think prompted the sudden move? Surely they could have found ways to make money in Europe."

Emilie smiled at him. "Perceptive. They're after the Jewel of the Sea."

Rafe frowned. "Am I supposed to know what that is?"

She slipped a photo over to him of a brilliant diamond. "This is the Jewel of the Sea. It's worth over

$25 million now. It's a Vandergraff family heirloom from their mother. She was some kind of countess or something. She came from an old family name without much liquid wealth but with a title and lands and all that jazz. That diamond is passed on from mother to daughter. It vanished right around the time of Dieter Vandergraff's death."

And there it was—the tickle along the nape of his neck that told him all was not right with his fucked-up world. Rafe kept his voice even. "So, what do you want from me?"

"Everything you have on them. Comb your old files. If these two are here, it's problematic for all of us."

He gave her a sharp nod. "I'll look through what I have and give ORUS a call. Most of the files you're after would have been under the old leadership and not available to us. But I'll ask." For now he'd leave out that he had access to those files.

She gave him a smile that was all teeth. She didn't trust him. *Well, that goes both ways, sister.*

"You do that. Before you go though, are you sure you were entirely forthcoming about that night you were there?"

So it was like that? Good thing he'd been trained to do nothing but lie. After all, survival depended on it. "Absolutely. You know what I know."

She nodded. "Okay then, I'd love to take a look at whatever files you can dig up. You know, fresh eyes and all that."

The hell he'd give her ORUS files without redacting them first. Interpol had been less than successful trying to get in with ORUS. Since the new leader was currently an ally of sorts, he sure as shit wasn't giving Emilie Durand her in. "Of course. If we're done, I'm out."

She slid her glance over him again. "I understand that you're pseudo retired. Care to share what you're up to these days?"

He grinned. "Nope." Turning his attention back to Alan, he nodded. "I'll get you what you need."

RAFE TOOK the same underground pass he usually took, then went through a series of checkpoints that led to the exit. From there, he deliberately took over an hour to get home. Just to make sure he wasn't tailed. Before he'd 'come back from the dead,' he'd been stationed in Philly. But after his miraculous resurrection, he'd moved back to New York to be closer to Lulu.

And somehow he'd ended up with more family than he'd had in six long years. Granted, they might not all think of him as family. You try to kill some guys one time... and they held it against you.

He knew the drill. To most of the world, Rafe DeMarco was dead. If he didn't want to resurrect that ghost just yet, he still had to be careful. If the Vandergraffs were kicking up a fuss again, his old life might be coming back to haunt him.

On McMillan, the winding two-lane road he often used as an alternate route home, he saw taillights glowing in a ravine and frowned. What the hell?

He liked this route. It was an old access road that let him bypass the freeway. Technically it was only meant for government and Parks and Recreation access, but Noah had ways of bypassing pesky access rules.

The weather hadn't given way to spring yet, and as there weren't very many streetlights, the road was often dark and desolate. And with the added benefit of the rain that had started an hour ago, it was eerie.

He reached the embankment where the light shone brightest and stopped his car. Fuck balls, someone had gone over. "Hello? Is anyone down there?"

There was a faint rustling, and Rafe strained to hear better. Then he heard what he was looking for.

"Help."

Shit. "Are you hurt?" He couldn't see a fucking thing thanks to the rain. He *could* see the steam rising up from somewhere down off the embankment, but very little else. All he heard was that voice.

"I'm hurt, but I can walk. I climbed out of the car."

"Visibility is shit right now, so I need you to move closer to the lights. I'm coming down for you."

There was a pause of silence. "Don't be ridiculous. Just call for help or something. You come down here and we'll both be stuck trying to climb up a mudslide."

Rafe's lips twitched. "Have a little faith, would you?"

"I have plenty of faith in AAA. The fire department even. Not some random wannabe hero."

Even with the rain dripping into his face and the cold air puffing out of his lungs, he had to stifle a laugh. "Listen, lady, you want to stay down there longer than you have to? It's cool. I'll call the fire department, and we'll wait the extra twenty minutes it will take them to get out here. Or I can come and get you now, and by the time they get here, you'll already be safe. Then it will just be a rescue mission for your car. I mean, it's cold and rainy, but it's really up to you."

There was another beat of silence. And then her voice came again, this time sounding as if she spoke through clenched teeth. "Okay, fine."

"See, I knew you could be reasonable. Give me one minute."

Rafe couldn't be sure, but he was pretty certain he heard her say, "You better know what you're doing."

He ran back to the driver's side and pulled his car up several feet, then threw it into park and engaged the hand brake. Next he ran to his trunk and pulled out his rappelling gear. He had his harness on in seconds. He just hoped she didn't ask too many questions about why the hell he had rappelling gear. What would he say to that? *Oh, you know, I just like to do a little building scaling on the weekends.* And this was why he could never have a normal life.

Once he had the harness on, he dropped the rope as close to the lights as possible. When he was secured in, he steadied himself on the ledge and stepped backward. Then, foot by foot, he dropped gently, calling out to the woman down below. She was right; the mud was slippery as hell. When he reached her, she was only a few feet up from where the car was. She wore only a thin dress, and her feet were bare.

Shit. She was lucky she didn't have hypothermia. "Hi. I'm Rafe. I'm going to help you out of here."

Even wet, shivering, and resembling a tiny drowned animal, she was beautiful. Those dark eyes of hers bore into him as she stared at him. "You were serious about coming down for me?"

Rafe rolled his eyes. "You know, as rescue-ees go, you

are a tad ungrateful." Rafe had the harness around her in seconds and wrapped his arm around her waist, pulling her close. He inhaled for a moment and caught a whiff of vanilla.

So not the right time to realize she was cute and smelled amazing. *Focus, man.*

Her lips twitched as she met his gaze. "Oh, I'm grateful. I just think you're crazy. You better have a whole army up there ready to pull us up. Because this mud—"

"Do you always talk this much?"

She opened her mouth, very likely to give him some kind of scathing retort, but then he pressed the electronic switch on his rope ascender and they were zooming up. Definitely not as fast as the system was capable of, given his weight and his rough approximation of hers, but it would do. He had to physically pull them up the last couple of feet, but she helped, mostly by not getting in the way and just clinging to him tightly.

Once they were on solid ground, she still clung to him and Rafe let her. For several beats they stood like that, with her wrapped around him and him encasing her in his arms, giving her some of his warmth.

But then she pulled back. And that mouth of hers started again. "So, are we going to talk about why you have burglary equipment handy?"

Despite himself, he laughed. "So, this is you being

grateful? And for your information, I'm a rappeller. It's a sport." It was the best he could do in a pinch.

"This is me making sure I haven't been rescued by a serial killer."

Rafe rolled his eyes. "I promise you, I'm not Dexter. Why don't you sit in the car and warm up while we wait for an ambulance to come and check you out."

Her eyes went wide. "I'm fine. I don't need an ambulance. Just point me in the direction of downtown, and I have it from here."

"Are you crazy? It's miles to Manhattan."

She squared her shoulders. "So? I'm strong. Thank you very much for your rescue or whatever. But I can take it from here."

Rafe stared down at her. She was tiny. At least compared to him. "You're insane if you think I'm going to let you walk. And have you not noticed that you're barefoot?"

She looked at her feet and wrapped her arms around herself. "I'm fine. I don't need your help. I'll just call an Uber or something."

Rafe stared at her. "Oh yeah? With what phone?"

She narrowed her gaze at him but stayed silent. When she turned her back on him and started walking in the wrong direction, he fought an inner battle with himself. The fact that she didn't want medical attention and was insistent on walking away from this told him she was in trouble. And the last thing he needed was trouble in his life.

The problem was, as soon as she was ten feet away from him, he was calling after her. "Hey. Let me give you a ride."

She turned to face him. "Thank you, Rafe. But I have this."

He chuckled low. "So, is now a good time to tell you you're walking in the wrong direction?"

And then he saw it, the telltale quiver of her bottom lip. *Shit.* She was about to cry. He strode up to her and wrapped her in his arms. There was a reason he kept his life simple. There was a reason he stayed alone. The problem was this girl slid under all his defenses. He knew he shouldn't take her home. But she clearly needed help. Besides, it wasn't like he didn't have the best security in the world. She was one tiny girl. How much damage could she really do?

"Look, something tells me you're in trouble."

"I am not in trouble. I just need somewhere to lay low for a while."

He sighed. "Fair enough. Come with me. Although, if you're going to crash in my spare room, I should probably know your name."

She blinked wide, dark eyes up at him. "It's Diana. Diana Renquist."

HAD it really been that easy?

Granted, considering Diana had dragged herself through mud and had nearly gotten hypothermia from the chilly rain, it hadn't exactly been *easy*.

But Rafe had done exactly as predicted. Months of watching him had paid off. And now she was in the den of a killer.

How evil can he be? He stopped to help a total stranger. She shut that shit right down. That was her traitor of a vagina talking.

Of course she knew how good-looking he was. But it was nothing compared to having him wrapped around her as he held her in the harness and lifted them out of the ravine. His scent still lingered on her, sending tingles to parts of her body she refused to think with.

What she hadn't expected was for him to bring her home... to his house. The plan had been to get him to take her to a hotel, give him the cover story, compel him to come back and check on her, and snare him with her feminine wiles. Whatever the fuck those were. But he'd taken her home.

Who does that? She could be a serial killer for all he knew.

Her rib still hurt like hell. The pain radiated down her side. Every now and again, she'd turn too quickly and send searing pain all the way down to her hip.

She sensed Rafe before he spoke and turned to face him as he entered the bedroom he'd given her.

"You feel better after the shower?"

Diana nodded. "Yes. Thank you. I didn't realize how cold I was. If I'd thought it through properly, I probably should have grabbed my coat from the car when I scrambled out." More like she'd tossed it when she heard him coming for her. *This is a mistake.* No. Desperate times called for desperate measures. He'd killed her father.

"Do you have any idea how fortunate you are? I mean, you could've died on impact. Not to mention that I came along when I did on such a desolate stretch of road. You must have one hell of a lucky charm."

"I'm not really a lucky kind of girl." She dropped her gaze to her hands. She deliberately didn't look up at him until he spoke again. She had to work hard to pull off the wary, downtrodden thing. She'd learned a long time ago it was better to meet men's gazes directly. They were less likely to fuck with you if you did. *But this is not you.*

This was Diana Renquist. She needed to put on that persona like a suit.

He held out a T-shirt and a pair of shorts for her. “These should do for now. I just put your clothes in the wash so you’ll have them for tomorrow at least. In the morning, we’ll figure out what your next steps will be.”

She took the clothes from him. “Thank you for this. I know I was kind of a pain in the ass. I’m just not used to people helping me.”

Rafe nodded, then turned his back. There was an awkward pause before Diana figured out he was giving her some privacy to change, although he didn’t leave the room. Quickly she scrambled into the clothes, hissing slightly as she pulled the shirt down.

He whipped around at the sound, just in time to catch her as she pulled the edge of the T-shirt past her ribs.

His brows dropped into an immediate scowl. “That bruise from the crash?”

She lowered her gaze. That would certainly explain it, but what if he knew about injuries and shit? Would the lie pass muster? And well, if he thought someone did it to her, it would certainly tie in to her cover story.

When she didn’t respond, his voice dropped an octave, but somehow instead of going warm and flowing over her like liquid, it went icy and deadly. "Did someone do that to you?"

Oh, protective are you? Where was this protective instinct with my father? She licked her lips. "It's not a big deal."

"The hell it isn't. Who did that to you? Is that the reason you were trying to walk to the city?"

She tilted her chin up. "Look, I am grateful. I really am. You're right. I could have died down in that ravine. But you came along. You did the whole Good Samaritan thing. But not everyone is like you."

Wasn't that the truth? Along the way, she'd met better than him. And worse. He was just the asshole at the top of her list.

"There are guys out there who don't think twice about hitting a woman. Unfortunately, I happened to meet one of those. And he did this." That much was the truth. What she left out was that she'd gotten in a good groin kick as retaliation. "It won't be happening again." Yeah, she'd bet the fucker had learned some control now.

The look in his golden eyes was murderous, and a chill ran over her skin. There he was. The killer she knew he was didn't linger too far below the surface.

She shivered as she remembered the first night she'd seen him. He'd had the darkest eyes she'd ever seen, almost black. Those vampire eyes had haunted her nightmares for years. Well, now she was about to be the stuff of *his* nightmares.

But he didn't hurt you.

Again, she shoved down that voice. Never mind that he looked good enough to lick. *Stupid vagina, there's a reason you're not consulted on these types of things.*

One thing though… she'd always wondered why he'd left her alive. It would have been cleaner to kill her. After all, she'd seen him. Though she hadn't seen his face. Why had he just left her in a closet when she was so obviously a loose end? She wasn't supposed to be home that night, but the friend she was meant to stay with had gotten sick. Her brothers had been gone. It had been just her and her father in the study.

That's what she needed to remember. Despite the fact that he hadn't hurt her then, despite the fact that he'd rescued her today, Rafe DeMarco was a monster. It was hard to reconcile. At the same time, he looked capable of murder right now.

"Tell me his name," he said quietly.

She shook her head. "No. I just want to leave that part of my life behind. I took everything I had when I left. Of course, now it's all at the bottom of the ravine. Hell, I don't even have any shoes."

He frowned as he asked, "What were you planning to do?"

Diana bit her lip. She had a cover story ready. But she didn't want to oversell it.

"I ran out and just started driving. I figured I'd lay low. Find a place to stay, get a job. I've been doing odd jobs and stuff since I graduated, so I'm trying to find myself anyway. Basically, I just needed to disappear for a minute."

Rafe leveled an intense stare at her, as if he was trying to decipher the lies from the truth. "Okay. You'll lay low here for as long as you need. In the morning we'll head to the store and grab you the basics so you'll at least have shoes."

She shook her head. "No. You don't need to do that. Besides, I can't really go to the store *without* shoes. I can order stuff online. My accounts are tied to my credit cards, so at least I won't be a burden for more than a place to stay. I'll call my card companies in the morning and get them to send me replacements, I guess."

This was all part of the show. This had been in the works for over a year. The fake ID she had procured came complete with a credit history and a previous rental history, just in case Rafe checked.

"I don't mind."

"You've been generous enough, just letting me stay here." She lifted her chin. "I can take care of myself."

"Well, maybe you shouldn't have to." He held her gaze for a long moment, and something unexpected happened... Butterflies fluttered low in her belly.

What the hell? No. And this is why we don't bring a vajayjay to a gunfight. Time to gird her loins.

Just because the guy was being nice now didn't mean she could be attracted to him. This man was a killer. He had killed her father. Hell, he looked about ready to kill her fictitious boyfriend right now.

"Thank you. For everything. As soon as I have my cards and stuff, I'll be out of your way."

He shrugged and shoved his hands into his jeans. "Something tells me it won't be so bad to have you around for a while." He inclined his head toward the door. "I'm just down the hall if you need anything. The kitchen is to the left. I put out some soup on the counter. Figured you might be hungry. I'm not much of a cook, but I have a housekeeper and she leaves food for me."

"Thank you. Again. You really don't have to do all this."

His lips twitched into a semblance of a smile. "Do you have to argue with me about everything?"

"Yep. It makes things more interesting."

Rafe barked out a laugh. "Okay, fair enough. Get some rest. Everything will look better tomorrow."

When he was gone, she sagged with relief. Holy hell. It was one thing to rehearse and research and watch him from afar. It was a whole other thing to face him. He was just a man. A good-looking assassin guy who rappelled down random ravines to save women he didn't even know. Her problem was he came across as really sincere and decent. But she knew it was a lie. She'd have to watch herself with him. If he was this good of a liar, no doubt he was an expert at spotting liars. She'd have to be careful.

She ate in the kitchen alone and washed up. But she waited an hour before she dared to venture into the rest of the condo. When they'd first arrived, he took her directly to the enormous guest bathroom, handed her a robe and towels, and pulled out shampoos and soaps for her.

Admittedly, she'd taken her sweet time in the shower. He had one of those multiple-head showers that pretty much massaged her whole aching body. On her ribs, that had hurt, but when she'd angled her body away from the main showerhead, everything else felt like heaven.

The kitchen opened up to a massive great room on the left. And on the right was a room with an arched entryway. She had noted the discreetly placed security cameras when they'd first arrived. This condo was all white and gray and steel. Very modern. Lacking warmth. Very much a bachelor pad. But the taste was impeccable if not cold.

Feet bare, padding across the kitchen floor, Diana walked toward the room on the right. On the walls, there were several pieces of art. If he was hiding something, these pieces would be the perfect cover for a safe.

But before she even had a chance to look behind the first one, she heard footsteps. Or maybe she imagined those? She went to touch the picture frame again, and then she saw the telltale shadow.

Whipping around, she swallowed a squeak. "Oh my God. You scared me."

Rafe leaned against the entryway to the room. He wore nothing but pajama bottoms that hung low on his hips.

Holy hell.

The man was, in a word, *ripped*. She stared at his chest for a long moment before gathering her thoughts.

"Sorry, I got a glass of water and I was just trying to get the lay of my surroundings." She nodded toward the painting. "Is that a Daniel Decker? It's beautiful. It almost looks like an original."

Rafe nodded slowly. "It *is* an original."

Diana stared at him. He had a freaking *original* Daniel Decker painting? The British artist had come into fashion in the late eighties. It was said the royal family even had one of his pieces. There was no way someone normal owned a Daniel Decker. They went for hundreds of thousands of dollars.

"Oh shit. I didn't mean to touch the frame. I assumed—"

His lips did that twisting half-smile thing again, and her skin flushed warm. Okay, him smiling at her was going to be a problem. She had to get a handle on her response to him. He wasn't the first man to ever smile at her.

Yeah, but he's the first one to look this good.

"It's okay. I have motion sensor alarms set for the living room. I should have warned you. The moment you set foot in here, you set off one of them. You can get as close to the painting as you like."

"Holy cow," she muttered. "Motion sensors. Wow. Though, I guess with an original Daniel Decker, you probably should have motion sensors. You should probably get a whole like laser-beam situation going."

And again with that smile. "Would you crawl under it like Catherine Zeta-Jones?"

For a full two seconds, she stared at him. Was he flirting? Because her body certainly thought he was flirting, the way she practically melted into a puddle of hormones. "While I do enjoy a pair of good yoga pants, I'm not quite so desperate to get a look at a Daniel Decker. If I'd known, I'd have peered in here through the dining room."

"No big deal. The painting belonged to my parents."

"Wow. Were your parents in the mob?"

His laugh was rich and deep, and it poured over her like warm brandy. "No. It's actually a pretty cool story. My father won the painting in a card game. He and my mom died when I was sixteen. This and an Abigail Noir photo are the only things of value they left behind. My grandmother refused to sell them even when money was tight."

"I'm so sorry. Here I am opening up old wounds."

"It's okay. It was a long time ago. Come on. I'll take you back to bed."

Why, oh why, did her synapses fry at the sound of that? *No, you idiot, he doesn't mean he's taking you back to his bed.*

She had to get a grip. Because as attractive as he was, it was never going to happen. And before this was all over, she was going to lie, cheat, and steal from him to get her answers.

4

As far as hospitality went, Rafe figured he wouldn't win any awards. But he'd made sure his guest was comfortable, making up the bed in the spare room that he'd never used with the sheets that were still in the package. But Diana hadn't seemed to mind. In fact, she'd been asleep as soon as her head hit the pillow, looking for all the world like a small, wounded animal.

Rafe had stood there just staring at her for an embarrassingly long time. There was something... *compelling* about her. His secondary senses itched, poking holes in her story. But for the first time in a long time, he didn't want to examine things too closely.

I'm tired, he thought. Years of assuming the worst took their toll. For once he wanted to believe that someone was exactly what they presented themselves to be. Not everyone was a killer out to get him. This girl needed his help.

Now that it was the next morning, he was prepared for the gut punch he got every time he looked at her. He knocked lightly and then pushed the door open to see her sitting up in bed. Her blond hair was wild, and she had lines from the pillow marking up her face. She was a mess.

And the most beautiful thing I've ever seen.

Flustered at the thought, Rafe looked down at the bottle of painkillers in his hand and the plate with toast and jam. Irrationally, he wanted to hide it and then go find her something better. Despite the dirt and the cheap, thin dress he'd found her in yesterday, this was the kind of woman that screamed royalty. She would belong in some medieval castle being watched over by knights in shining armor. Which definitely didn't apply to him.

His armor had been tarnished long ago.

The thought made him feel stupid, so he thrust the bottle of aspirin at her. "I brought you some medicine. I should have brought you some before."

Her smile felt like watching the sunrise. Rafe was taken off guard by the heat blossoming inside him just from the thought that he'd pleased her in some way.

"Thank you. I feel a little better, but I'll take some

anyway. I hit my head along the way." Her face darkened then, and Rafe wondered what memory had triggered such an intense look.

"We can see about getting your car towed out today. Although it looked pretty bad, so it's probably totaled."

Diana sighed. "I figured it was. That's about how my life is going lately."

She looked around, and he realized belatedly that if he was going to bring her aspirin, he should have brought her a glass of water too.

Way to go, playboy. You definitely know how to take care of a woman.

She stood and stretched, and Rafe could see the imprint of her nipples through the thin fabric of the T-shirt he'd given her to sleep in. He swallowed hard and averted his gaze, though every cell in his body was unhappy about the decision.

"So, I've got some extra sweats and stuff you can wear and flip-flops. I just tossed all my T-shirts and stuff in the wash and my sweatshirts will drown you, so you might have to wear the same T-shirt out. I know you said your cards will be coming, but I figured you'd feel better with some clothes that fit and some shampoo and stuff you like."

Her lip quivered, and he shifted uncomfortably on his feet. Shit. Was he this fucking out of practice?

"I don't know what to say."

He chose levity to try to dissipate some of the tension. "That's a first."

A bark of laughter tore out of her chest, then she immediately winced and placed tentative fingers to her jaw. "You know you might be right about that. For once I'm listening to what my father used to say. 'If only your ears were your tongue, how much more useful they would be.'"

Rafe shrugged. "I don't think so. Your mile-a-minute talking kinda grows on a person." He wanted to tell her not to bother being embarrassed, because she was beautiful and there were men who'd mortgage their soul for the chance to be near her. She was here to get herself together, and the last thing he wanted to do was make her uncomfortable.

Truthfully, there was a part of him that was furious she'd come home with him. It wasn't safe for a beautiful young woman to trust any man that she met on the street, even if he'd helped her. It was the kind of thing he used to lecture Lucia about, when he was still allowed to do that. He felt a momentary pang for what he'd lost. While he'd been halfway around the world, Lucia had grown up without him. She had Noah to lecture her on safety now.

"Actually, you know what, have this one. I'll go grab a

button-down." Before he thought about the wisdom of what he was about to do, Rafe stripped off the shirt he was wearing and handed it over to her.

Diana's eyes widened at the sight of his bare chest, and she blushed when their gazes locked for a moment before her attention returned to his torso. She looked away, but a few seconds later, her eyes came back to caress his bare skin. Rafe suddenly understood why so many men acted like idiots around women. He had the sudden urge to flex for her and maybe show off what all the finely honed muscle groups in his body could really do.

Yep, he could think of a perfect way to show all that off. *Fuck, get it together.*

"I should have brought you some water. I'll get you a glass."

That seemed to break Diana's concentration. "It's okay, I'm ready to get up anyway. I should probably get going. Lots to do today."

She followed him out of the room, carrying the plate with the toast on it. He heard the crunch as she bit into it. By the time they reached the kitchen, the plate was empty.

"Hungry?" He grinned and then pulled down a glass from the cabinet and filled it with water from the refrigerator.

Diana laughed. "A little. That soup I had last night seems like it was a long time ago."

Rafe's attention was drawn to the way she favored her left side. He'd done that plenty of times himself when he was injured.

"How are your ribs?"

She looked startled and then took a gulp from the glass. "It's no big deal. I'm fine."

Oh hell, she was a bad liar. Rafe couldn't decide if that was a good thing or a bad thing.

"So you probably have to go to work today. I'll get out of your way."

Rafe grabbed her hand before she could move. "You don't have to leave. I work from home a lot. Besides, we'll hit the shops first."

"Work from home? That's convenient. What do you do?"

He decided to stick with his standard cover story. "I'm in security. Pretty boring actually. I deal with personnel issues."

She narrowed her eyes like she didn't believe him, but Rafe didn't even blink. *I have a hell of a lot more practice lying than you do, sweetheart.*

"Well, I should probably still go. I'm sure you have stuff to do. You don't need me hanging around."

"Shopping, remember?" Rafe tugged on one of the blond curls hanging over her shoulder.

"You're really not going to let that go, are you? Are you always this stubborn?" She smiled, but it turned to a grimace. Rafe slid an arm underneath her and carried her to the couch.

"Short answer, yes."

"What are you doing?" she protested.

Rafe ignored her and walked back to his bathroom to get the arnica cream he used for his own bruises. He felt calmer by the time he got back, but that calmness disappeared when he lifted the edge of the shirt she was wearing and he cursed a blue streak. He took a deep breath, trying to move past the rage he felt at seeing the large purple bruise on the right side of her torso. There was no hiding it. She'd been punched or kicked in the ribs recently.

"You probably need to be seen by a doctor. He could have killed you." Even before she started shaking her head, he figured that wouldn't go over well. "Well, you at least need to take it easy over the next few days."

"I have so much to do. Finding a place, getting a job."

"All of that can wait. You're welcome to stay here and keep me company."

Suddenly Diana wouldn't look at him. When she finally turned, he saw her swiping away tears.

"It's just so embarrassing, you know? I never thought he would..."

"Hit you?" Rafe finished for her. They didn't speak as he smoothed the cream gently over the bruise.

To give himself time to settle, he walked back to the kitchen to wash his hands. All the while his mind was going in a million directions, but they all led to the same road. Who was the fucker who'd hurt her, and how many ways could Rafe make him beg before he put him out of his misery? He walked back into the living room and knelt next to the couch.

"You have nothing to be embarrassed about. You didn't do anything wrong. Any chance you'll make it easier for me and just tell me his name?"

Diana focused on his face then, her dark eyes probing his. "Not a chance. I have a feeling if I told you that, he wouldn't make it through the night. And I'm not interested in blood being shed in my name, thanks."

"You have good instincts then. Because I was thinking he wouldn't make it through breakfast." When her dark eyes flared wide, he forced a smile onto his face. "Let's get you ready, then we'll get you some new clothes."

Their eyes met, dark into dark, before she finally sighed. "Okay, I guess I can hang around for a little while."

Rafe didn't reply, just nodded and went back to his room to change. Diana didn't know it yet, but she'd be hanging around a lot longer than a little while.

Because he didn't plan on letting her out of his sight until he knew she was safe.

RAFE DIDN'T REALIZE the flaw in his plans until the next day.

After spending the previous day shopping with her and sleeping on the situation for a night, he realized having her so close wasn't going to be easy.

He'd never had a woman in his apartment before. Especially not one that fired his protective senses the way Diana did.

Yeah great job, asshole. The last thing an injured woman needs is you going all Captain America on her behalf.

But reining in his murderous rage at the sight of that huge bruise on her ribs would have been impossible.

On a high note, she was still talking to him. So she wasn't entirely freaked out. The problem was she kept giving him those eyes. The ones that said she wanted him to lose it on her behalf. The ones that beckoned him closer when he knew he needed to stay away. He wasn't the kind of guy she needed.

She needed someone kind and sensitive. And he was far from that. He was all rough edges and a killing machine. He'd been out in the cold too long.

But as he started to get ready to leave for Lucia's, a niggling sense of guilt and longing pricked at him. He didn't want to leave her by herself. She was still hurt. *Oh, who are you kidding? You want to hang out with her.*

His dick twitched in his jeans and Rafe growled. "Down, boy." Now was not the time.

He didn't have room in his life for a relationship. Nor was he that guy. As much as he wanted her, he wasn't an idiot.

It had been a while since he'd been on a real date. But last he remembered, women didn't want to be with killers. They wanted nice picket-fence-type things. Like his sister.

Your sister's with a killer.

Yes, but Noah had changed. He wasn't exactly domesticated, but he didn't have the same sharp edges that he used to have. Rafe wasn't even sure that was possible for him.

He didn't have time for this. If he didn't get moving soon, he'd be late. Ever since he'd come back from the dead, he treasured the time he could spend with his family. He paused as he passed Diana's room and hesitated at the door. What if she was asleep? He'd told her to go and rest.

Stop being a pussy and knock.

Before he could, the door swung open and Diana took a step back at the sight of his raised fist.

"Shit! I mean, sorry. I was coming to say goodbye." Rafe had never felt more like a flustered teenager, stammering and sweating when he spoke to a pretty girl.

The thought made him stand straighter. He was known for his icy control. Losing focus was a good way to get a knife in your back. Just because he wasn't in the game anymore didn't mean he could afford to get sloppy.

"Right. Of course. You probably have a million things to do."

Guilt pricked at him again. Maybe he should invite her along. It felt wrong to go out and leave her to fend for herself. However, he was going to visit his family, and despite how she got under his skin, he wouldn't bring someone unknown around the most precious people in his life.

"Just need to run a few errands. Anything you need while I'm out?"

She shrugged. "No, I'm good. Actually, I'm really tired already. Which is ridiculous since all I've done is eat breakfast and take a shower. But... yeah."

Her hand fluttered unconsciously to her ribs and Rafe realized she was probably in pain.

"There's more painkiller in the bathroom cabinet. Just in case."

She grunted noncommittally, so he could only hope she wouldn't let pride stop her from taking them.

Not your problem either way.

With a little wave, Rafe headed out, making sure to lock the door behind him. The sight of her little wince stayed with him as he rode the elevator down to the parking garage and on the drive over to the penthouse that served as headquarters for Blake Security.

But as soon as the elevator opened on the top floor, his attention was diverted by the sight of Lucia holding his niece.

When she saw him, Lucia let out a little squeal that startled the baby.

"Rafe! You're here. I didn't know you were coming."

He grinned, unable to conceal the thread of pure joy that wrapped around his throat every time he saw her. Especially now, seeing her all grown up and so happy. She'd been a sweet kid who had grown into a lovely woman. And now she was a mother.

"Hey, Lulu. Noah asked me earlier to come by." He leaned down so she could kiss his cheek.

When he got close, he turned his head to kiss Lucia

on the forehead and then placed a soft kiss on top of Isabella's head. She blew a spit bubble and waved her chubby little legs in excitement.

"Look, Izzy. Uncle Rafe is here," Lucia cooed in a soft voice.

He took her from Lucia and sighed as the baby curled trustingly against his chest. If pressed, Rafe would always say that Lucia was the most beautiful baby he'd ever seen, but he couldn't deny that Isabella was a close second. She'd gotten the intense dark hair of her father combined with her mother's big gray eyes. Then, somehow, despite not being blood related, she seemed to have gotten the mischievous nature of her almost-Aunt JJ. Which was evidenced when she suddenly sat straight up and held out her arms to someone standing behind him.

"Look, Matthias. She missed you," Lucia commented.

Rafe turned and nodded to the kid. Matthias usually only talked to him when absolutely necessary and didn't pretend to like him. It was the type of honesty that Rafe respected. He passed the baby carefully, noticing that whereas Izzy had been on the verge of going to sleep in his arms, she was wide awake as she stared up at Matthias.

Then they all smelled it.

"Oh, bugger," Matthias muttered. "Every time. It's like she saves it for me."

Lucia looked like she was trying not to laugh. "Um, well, at least she's comfortable with you!" She took Izzy back and waved over her shoulder as she headed for the nursery. "I'll be right back."

Matthias glanced at him briefly. "Noah's on his way up."

Rafe rocked back on his heels and let out a slow breath. It was odd, being part of the family yet still on the outside. Noah and Lucia had built something together that he would never truly be a part of, and he was happy they had. They'd fashioned a true family filled with people with ties even tighter than blood. It was something that had taken years to build, years that he hadn't been there. Nothing could change that, but at least he knew his sacrifices had been worth it.

Lucia would never be alone again.

"Hey, you could have come back." Noah appeared at his elbow, looking stressed and tired.

"I didn't want to intrude. You mentioned you needed something."

Noah glanced at Matthias before nodding. "Yeah, I didn't want to talk about it over the phone." He handed Rafe a slip of paper bearing a name that Rafe didn't recognize.

"This piece of shit has been slippery as fuck. He keeps a very low profile online, which is why Matthias is having trouble tracking him. But no one does old-school tracking like you do."

Rafe grinned. It made him feel a million years old to have the methods he'd been trained in described as "old school," but there was definitely value to the manual methods. Plenty of people avoided leaving an online footprint, particularly because of how easy it was to track. But no matter how careful this guy was, it was impossible to exist without leaving some trace. He had to eat. He had to rest his head somewhere at night.

And when he did, Rafe would find him.

"I'll take care of it."

Lucia appeared again with Isabella changed into a fresh onesie. "Okay, let's try this again. I wouldn't want her to miss her uncle fix. No one calms her like you do, Rafe."

He accepted the baby back and, for the next hour, walked around the penthouse murmuring softly to her. Seeing that her daughter was sound asleep, Lucia left to finish some laundry, which made Rafe think of Diana. He should get back and check on her. Take her to get something to eat.

"I've gotta go. Can you let Lucia know that I'll be back tomorrow?"

Matthias nodded and took the baby. When she sighed and didn't wake, he looked relieved.

Right before the elevator doors closed, he heard Matthias's soft curse.

"Bloody hell. She's soiled her nappy again?"

5

The next day, Diana waited for about ten minutes after Rafe left before she jumped out of bed and started searching the apartment again. She'd learned her lesson the prior day. He'd been gone such a short time that he'd almost caught her inspecting the windowsills.

She couldn't afford that kind of error again. This morning he'd said he was going out for some groceries to make breakfast, so she was pretty sure it would take him at least half an hour even if he only got a few things.

As she pulled open drawer after drawer, she was struck again by how sparse everything was. If she had to guess, she'd think he'd only just moved in instead of having been here for years.

Her fingers lifted to the chain around her neck. The half-dollar was tarnished as hell after all these years, but it wasn't about what it looked like. Every time she touched it, she could almost hear her father's voice. *Luck comes to the bold, Diana. If you want it, then you have to go and get it.*

She breathed through the pain of missing him, an ache that might go dormant for weeks and then return with a vengeance that could take her to her knees. Over the years, she'd heard so many platitudes about death. It gets easier with time. Time heals all wounds. It was all bullshit. Because no matter how much time passed, she was still alone. Left with no parents, and brothers who regularly forgot she existed.

And there was no way to heal that.

No, there was no healing in her future. But there was something that would make her feel better—getting revenge on the one who'd torn her world apart.

The thought galvanized her, and she moved faster. When she'd staged the crash, she'd known then that she couldn't take anything with her, so she'd left her actual valuables in the long-term hotel room she'd booked under an alias. Eventually she'd go retrieve her things. But for now, appearing helpless and needy worked in her favor.

If she'd gotten his psychology right, Rafe wouldn't allow her to leave but instead would ask her to stay under his protection until he was sure she was okay. She shook her head. It was such a strange thing that there were some violent men who believed in protecting women. It was the most oddly contradictory thing, but she'd observed it before.

I guess he doesn't feel the same obligation to be a protector when he's out killing men.

Diana growled at the thought and then walked to the kitchen to retrieve a plastic bag. Not that she had much to take with her, just the makeup and the outfits they'd picked up when Rafe took her out shopping.

Just as she got back to the bedroom, the door opened behind her, and she paused. What the hell? She'd been listening for him and hadn't heard a thing. It was a reminder of just what kind of man she was dealing with. Rafael DeMarco was not someone she could afford to underestimate.

"Hey, Diana." His eyes dropped to the plastic bag in her hand and his eyes narrowed. "What are you doing? You're leaving?"

The "without saying goodbye" hung unspoken in the air between them, and Diana almost felt guilty. Almost. His chivalrous streak had been a surprising yet helpful discovery. She hadn't counted on feeling guilty for playing on it though.

Imagine that, feeling guilty for playing with the feelings of a murderer.

Diana squared her shoulders. "You've done enough. I'm sure you don't need me hanging around any longer than necessary."

"You're not in the way at all. And I don't think you should be out there until you have a safe place to stay. You don't, do you?"

She didn't meet his eyes. *Keep it mild. Look sad.*

"That's really none of your business. You can't tell me what to do."

Rafe let out a frustrated growl. "You're right, I can't."

Immediately Diana started to panic. Had she gotten this wrong? She'd assumed he would insist that she stay as long as she wanted, but maybe she'd overplayed her hand. Damn it. If he let her leave, she wouldn't have the time she needed to search his place. She needed him to get comfortable leaving her alone in the apartment for extended periods of time.

"Thank you for what you did. I don't know if I really expressed how grateful I am. You could have just left me at the bottom of that ravine."

Rafe grimaced. "No, I couldn't have. You needed help. I gave it. It's what I do. Or at least, it's what I try to do."

Was that guilt on his face? Diana couldn't process the roiling emotions stirred up by his words. If he tried to help people, why hadn't he helped her father? Did it haunt him, the things he'd done and the people he'd hurt? Maybe that was why he was trying to help people now, to atone for his past. But either way, it wouldn't bring her father back.

"I still think you should stay," he continued. "But I can't force you. But I just have one question. The guy who did that." He pointed at her ribs. "Is he out there looking for you?"

Diana crossed her arms. "I know how to stay off the radar."

Surprisingly, he laughed. "Not denying that. But no matter where you go, he could find you. That won't happen here."

She pretended to think about it while inside she was smirking. Finally. She was in.

"I guess I could stay a little longer. If you're sure I'm not in the way."

"You're not in the way. Where were you even going to go?"

She shrugged. "A motel or something. I need to think about what to do next. My life is a bit of a shit show right now."

"Well, as someone with a PhD in shit shows, let me tell you that it's much easier to figure out what to do next when you're not listening to a methed-out guy next door coming down from a high. Or worried about whether someone will break in."

Diana laughed as she was sure he'd expected her to. "You're right. And I know I must seem ungrateful, but I really appreciate the room."

She dropped the plastic bag on the bed. "So did you get groceries?"

Rafe seemed more than happy to change the subject. "Yes, I did. Although I can't claim to be the best cook. You're going to have to settle for scrambled eggs and... scrambled eggs."

Diana shook her head. "At least I can be useful. Or at least I can do better than just eggs."

She followed him to the kitchen and gasped at the pile of plastic bags filled with groceries on the counter.

When she looked over at him, Rafe shrugged sheepishly. "You needed food. So I just got some of everything."

Determined not to be touched by the thoughtful gesture, Diana approached the counter. Just because she hated him didn't mean they both needed to starve.

"Today I have some work to do, so I'll be in my room for a while. Then later we have a party to go to."

"We?" Diana paused in the act of digging through the bags. She'd been counting on him leaving at some point so she could have more time to search the place. It bothered her that she hadn't seen any indication of a safe. He would have one, wouldn't he? Who stole a priceless jewel and then didn't put it in a safe? Unless he'd hidden it somewhere else. Maybe where they were going could provide a clue.

"A party, you say? Where?"

He put a carton of milk in the refrigerator before answering. "At my sister's place. It's just family, nothing fancy. But it should be fun, and the food will be amazing."

She kept her expression even as she mulled it over. It would cut into her time searching the apartment, but seeing his sister's place could yield clues. And if everyone there was busy talking, maybe they wouldn't notice her poking around.

"Sounds good. Now, how do you like your eggs?"

"Cooked," Rafe replied. "That's about as picky as I get."

Diana picked up a spatula. "Okay then." She hated to admit it, but if she didn't hate Rafael DeMarco so much, she'd probably like him.

WITH A DEEP BREATH, Rafe knocked on the door, waiting until he heard her soft response before opening it.

Diana lounged on the bed, reading one of the thrillers from his bookshelf.

"Are you ready to go?"

Diana sat up so fast the book fell to the ground. "Already? I figured it would be at nighttime."

"No, it's actually a birthday party, so it's in the afternoon. We have time if you want to change or... do girl stuff."

Her lips twitched. "I probably should. I'm sure your family will wonder why you're bringing some girl who looks like she was on the losing end of a boxing match."

Fucking hell. He hadn't even considered that she might not feel well enough to go. "I should have asked how you were feeling first. Sorry. If you're sore, we don't have to go. We can stay here and hang out."

Diana looked at him strangely. "You don't have to miss a family party because of me. Besides"—a light blush tinted her cheeks—"I'm okay. The ribs hurt a little bit less when I breathe in each day."

He wasn't sure how to respond. Was she just saying that so he wouldn't worry? He was severely out of practice at decoding woman-speak. Sure, he'd had relationships of sorts. But none ever lasted for more than a few months. And none of those women had ever known who he was or even a reasonable facsimile of the truth. Three months was usually the mark where it became too exhausting to lie all the time. Even when he was deep undercover and he had to fully believe the story of who he was, it was still hard to lie to someone you were supposed to trust. In the field, that saved your life. But out in the real world, that just destroyed you.

"Good. That's good then. But take your time getting ready. I didn't mean to rush you."

Another flush and she tucked a wayward blond lock behind her ear. "Oh. Yeah. Sure. Let me just maybe change into something a little nicer."

"You don't have to get dressed up or anything. It's just a birthday party. We're not formal people."

She shook her head. "Yes, I do. Men don't get it. I can't show up looking horrible. They'll wonder what's wrong with you taking in a stray."

Rafe stepped into the room and sat on the bed next to her. "You look great. And if I'm being honest, having you there will help me feel less nervous. Please come."

Who the hell was he? He wasn't used to asking anyone for anything. Usually what came out of his mouth when dealing with women were commands. *Do this. Come here. Let's go to bed.* He didn't have softness in him. But for her, it seemed he did.

She licked her lips, and Rafe's eyes pinned to the pink tip of her tongue. Instant heat flashed through his body. Shit, he really needed to get a handle on that.

"Look, it's not like that. Everyone will be cool. Besides, I don't want you sitting here cooped up and scared. I want you with me."

She licked her lips again, and he worked hard to stifle a growl. "You're sure no one will mind?"

"Are you kidding? My sister will very likely roll out the welcome mat for you."

She gave him a shy smile. "Okay. Give me ten minutes to change."

Much to his surprise, she appeared in the living room exactly eight minutes later. Rafe was used to a different measurement of time when dealing with women getting ready to go out. Usually ten minutes meant forty-five. But Diana was wearing the same dress, now laundered and dry, that he'd found her in.

She was quiet as he led her down to the parking garage. Rafe had no idea what to say, so they made the short drive in silence.

When they reached the Blake Security building, Diana peered up at the signage. "Wow. Glass and steel. Impressive. What are we doing here?"

"This is where the party is."

"At a security company?" Her brows shot up.

His lips twitched. "It's sort of a long story. My brother-in-law owns the place. Sort of a work-live situation."

"Okay then. Let's do this," she said with a sunny smile.

Rafe tried to match her enthusiasm, but nervous energy still flowed through his veins. When they reached the elevator, she slid her hand into his and squeezed. Her tiny, delicate hand gave him warmth, gave him strength. He tapped in the code to reach the penthouse and then leaned forward for the retinal scan. If Diana thought that was strange, she said nothing.

When the elevator doors pinged, he sucked in a deep breath. Next to him, Diana squeezed his hand and gave him a bright smile. "It will be fine. Watch. I have a feeling about these things."

They were met in the foyer by Oskar, whose permanent scowl was in place.

"Oskar, how's it going?"

"You're here, so not great." The German turned his attention to Diana, and his whole countenance changed as he suddenly plastered a wide smile on his face.

Rafe had to mutter under his breath. "Okay, I get you. Turn the wattage down."

His sometimes friend just laughed. "What's the matter, afraid of a little competition?" Oskar looked back to Diana. "So, are you going to introduce me to my future wife?"

Diana just laughed. "Are you always this outrageous?"

Oskar nodded. "Pretty much. I'm not as bad as Noah though. So, Rafe, you can thank your lucky stars."

Rafe pursed his lips. He was happier when the German was his usual scowling self. When he smiled, it made him almost appear charming.

"Okay, that's enough. Diana, this is Oskar. He works with my brother-in-law."

The German grinned again. "When you get tired of this guy, come find me."

Diana giggled, and Rafe tugged her behind him. He found Noah in the kitchen, attempting to molest his sister, who was laughing as he copped a feel. "Seriously, do you guys have to do that? There are people around."

Lucia laughed and pushed Noah away before rushing over to give him a hug. It didn't matter that he worked here now and she saw him almost every day, she always hugged him like she was trying to make up for all the days they'd missed.

He held her tight. It was still weird as hell to see Noah with his sister. Yeah, sure, he'd always loved the guy like a brother. But him and Lucia... Rafe had never even considered it an option. And now they were happily married and parents of the only other person who had him wrapped around her little finger more than Lucia—his niece, Isabella.

Noah came over and gave him a one-armed clap and then a good thump on the back. "What's up, brother?" He inclined his head and slid his gaze to Diana while Lucia was dancing from foot to foot. Oh boy. They were going to make this a big deal.

"Guys, this is Diana. She's a friend of mine. Diana, this is Noah Blake and my sister, Lucia."

Noah shook her hand briefly and welcomed her to the party. Lucia was far more exuberant and hugged her tight before taking her hand and dragging her out of the kitchen, talking a mile a minute.

Noah turned his attention back to Rafe. "A *friend*?"

Rafe just shrugged. "I do occasionally have those."

Noah narrowed his gaze and studied him for a long moment. Then he started to laugh. "Friends. Uh-huh."

Rafe shook him off. "Shut up."

"I never thought I'd see the day Rafe DeMarco—" He paused. "Does she know who you are? Or are you using an alias?"

Rafe shook his head. "No alias. I'm out, remember?"

Noah nodded. "So, *this* is new then."

"*This* is nothing. She's just a friend. That's all."

Noah chuckled. "Yeah, you just go ahead and tell yourself that." His friend clapped him on the back and said, "Come on, I just got the text from Dylan. Nonna will be here in ten minutes."

Rafe tried to make small talk. But his gaze kept tracking Diana. Lucia had commandeered her. And JJ, Lucia's best friend, was regaling her with stories of when they were young. He could only pray that JJ didn't give away all his dirt. But given that Diana was laughing, they were probably staying away from him as a topic.

He hoped.

DIANA ACCEPTED another glass of punch and tried to tune back in to the conversation. Lucia had made sure she was introduced to everyone, and her brain was swimming with all the names. But after a few minutes, it didn't seem to matter. Everyone included her in the conversation, so she didn't feel like an interloper at all.

To her surprise, Rafe's family seemed... nice.

It was a startling and incongruous thing that actually made her feel a little grumpy. Every part of her was uncomfortable with getting to know these women who talked about Rafe like some kind of superhero, knowing that she had every intention of exposing his crimes to the world. But now she was being forced to view the collateral damage of her plan. Rafe might be a murdering bastard, but he had family that loved him dearly. They'd be hurt once she got enough evidence to put him in jail. It didn't change what she had to do. Rafe needed to pay for his crimes. But she'd have to have ice water in her veins not to care that she'd be hurting nice people also.

As soon as she could, Diana excused herself and started toward the hallway she'd seen Lucia go down a few minutes ago. There had to be a bathroom back there. She needed a few minutes of quiet to get herself together. Rafe didn't trust her completely yet, but he wasn't threatened by her, obviously, or he wouldn't have brought her around his family. She needed to stay focused and get him to trust her enough to leave her in his apartment while he went to work.

This was no time to go soft. Not when she was so close to her target.

"Oh, shit! Sorry!" Diana skidded to a halt at the sight of Lucia and her husband wrapped around each other.

Lucia lifted her head, her eyes blurry. Noah didn't even acknowledge the interruption, burying his face in Lucia's neck while his hands lifted her higher. He stepped closer between her legs, pressing her against the wall.

"Okaaay... I'll just go back to the party now." Diana

laughed softly as the couple ignored her and continued attacking each other with their lips.

JJ met her at the end of the hallway. "Are you okay?"

"Oh fine. Totally fine."

The other woman gave her a strange look. "You're as red as a tomato. Let me guess, you caught Noah slobbing his wife down."

Diana choked. "Is that a common occurrence around here?"

"Yes. All the time. Not that I can talk, but at least my boyfriend and I keep it behind closed doors." JJ shook her head and started down the hallway. The next thing Diana heard was her shouting, "Get a room, you guys!"

Just then there was a loud chime. What was that? As she walked to the foyer, she realized it was the elevator. She hadn't heard that noise when they'd ridden up.

A beautiful older woman stepped off the elevator, followed by a handsome young man who was holding several bags.

"Nonna!"

Someone rushed by her, and Diana turned to see Lucia walking toward the older woman. She carried a little girl with dark hair and big gray eyes. Diana recognized the baby from her surveillance.

"Hello, *bambina*. I brought your gnocchi and some tiramisu for the boys."

Lucia accepted a kiss and then suddenly turned, thrusting the baby into Diana's arms. On instinct, she clutched the little girl against her.

"Oh no, I don't really know anything about babies."

But even as she said it, the little girl cuddled against her chest and rested a tiny fist near her throat. Diana's heart clutched at the gesture.

"Look, she likes you. She's finicky about who she lets hold her. You know, they say children can sense a good person. I'm glad Rafe has a good woman in his life." Lucia squeezed her arm gently before following the man holding the bags of food.

"Rafe?" The older woman looked over at Lucia's words. But Lucia was already gone. Suddenly the older woman paused, and her eyes fixed on something across the room. Rafe.

"Oh. *Oh*. I didn't know you would be here."

Rafe came forward, his expression so painfully tender that Diana found it difficult to watch. Who was this man? He definitely wasn't the cynical, paranoid one she'd arrived with.

"Of course I'm here," Rafe murmured. "It's your birthday, Nonna. I couldn't miss that. I've missed too many already."

Nonna let out a happy cry and embraced him. "I

know you have, *bambino*. But you're back now. And so skinny! Well, I'll fix that."

Rafe leaned down into the hug, his eyes closing as she stroked his hair. Diana couldn't hear what he was saying to her, but she could read the love between the two, and it took her off guard. She hadn't had that. It twisted her up inside watching them. Her father had loved her; she knew that. But being gentle didn't come naturally to him. He'd wanted her to be smart and independent and not to need anyone. She hadn't gotten many hugs, though there had been pats on the back for a job well done before her father retreated back to his office. Her brothers weren't the demonstrative types either. Mainly they ignored her unless they needed something.

She'd figured that was just how most men were. They weren't as emotional as women. After a while she'd learned not to expect hugs or softness. The way to gain her father's love was by providing results. Straight As on her report card. Winning a tennis tournament. That was how to get acknowledgment or the rare smile.

But this, this unabashed joy flowing from one to the other, wasn't something she was familiar with. And the longing she felt watching it took her completely off guard.

"Ba, ba, ba, ba." The baby in her arms babbled and

blew a small spit bubble. Then she looked at Diana and grinned.

When Lucia appeared at her elbow, Diana handed the baby back and mumbled an excuse about needing the bathroom. But truthfully what she needed was a break.

She'd thought she knew everything she needed to know about Rafe from her research and her surveillance. But the man she was slowly getting to know wasn't anything like the stone-cold killer she'd come here expecting.

So which one was the real Rafe?

6

"You're sure you're okay? You're not hurting too bad?"

"Yes. I told you I'm fine. I'm just a little sore—it's nothing."

She'd been off all day. Well, off since pretty much yesterday. He'd been trying to figure it out. She'd seemed fine at the party. But now something wasn't right.

He lived downtown near Chelsea Piers. So that morning they'd taken a walk, grabbed breakfast at one of those trendy hipster spots. Like a normal—well, couple.

Except you're not a couple, are you? No, but you want to be, obviously. Dumb ass. But his point was, everything should have been fine. But it wasn't. Quiet introspection he could handle, but this felt different. It felt like brooding.

"Everyone was cool to you yesterday, right? Noah's a good kid, but sometimes he can be an asshole."

She shifted her gaze off the television to meet his. "No. Noah was perfectly nice."

"Did JJ say something? Listen, she's brash, but you know, she's pretty cool—"

She laughed. "I don't know. I kinda liked her. And I don't think she's brash. I think she's awesome. She really will say anything. I almost swallowed my chicken wing whole when she told Oskar that her dick was bigger than his."

Rafe threw his head back and laughed. "I don't doubt it."

"I swear, I'm fine. I'm just thinking, you know? Your family is lovely. So, so... nice. Normal. Which is weird."

Rafe frowned. "What, you expected a three-eyed, three-horned, giant purple people eater?"

"If you're referring to that giant purple vibrator JJ was talking about, then possibly."

Rafe chuckled. "JJ is hilarious. Next time ask her about risking her life in an apartment fire to save her fish. You should have seen Jonas's face when he realized she'd run back in to rescue that thing while she was practically naked."

He still couldn't believe that shit. Rafe had been worried about her once they'd gotten the alarm. But Jonas had been beside himself. Rafe had never seen the guy like that before. But then, when Jonas discovered what she'd run back into the apartment for, he'd about lost it.

"If you're sure things are okay, I'll just have to trust you." The hell he would. His instincts had served him well over the past fifteen years or so. Something was wrong, and he'd figure out what it was. He was nothing if not patient.

She sighed. "Okay. look. If you must know, I sort of walked in on Noah and Lucia you know..."

Rafe blinked. Had he heard that right? "Noah and Lucia you know..." And then it dawned on him. He wasn't sure his body had ever gone through simultaneous reactions like this before—the urge to throw up coupled with the urge to throw his head back and laugh. "Oh."

"Yeah. *Oh*. I mean, are they always like that?"

Rafe nodded. "Yeah, pretty much. I know you're probably pretty traumatized by the whole thing, but don't worry about it. We've all walked in on them. And I mean *all* of us. If it is traumatizing and awkward for you, imagine how it is for—"

His phone rang. It was rare that anyone called him.

If it was some kind of emergency, Noah would have sent the usual signal, a series of texts and rings that would let him know he was needed for trouble. No, in this case, his phone was just ringing. Which meant *Oskar*. He didn't even look at the screen when he picked it up. "What do you want?"

"Is that any way to treat a friend? Not a friend, your mentor even."

Rafe clenched his jaw. Noah had been on something the day he paired him with Oskar. One of Rafe's main jobs once they got some new recruits would be training them to be efficient. He would be training them to kill, but only if they had to. Oskar thought it was his job to train Rafe to *not* kill people. As if he needed lessons on that. He had been FBI after all. *Yeah, but you were also an assassin for hire.* Details.

"Don't make me repeat myself. You know how I get when I get angry."

There was a bit of silence. "You know what, come to think of it, I'm still mad at you for that."

"Get on with it."

"Ah, someone's testy. Does that mean I interrupted some get-it-on time? What's his name? Is he big and burly? I picture you with a bear type myself. But hey, I don't judge. Whatever tickles your fancy."

Rafe just rolled his eyes. Oskar had somehow gotten

it in his head that for six years Rafe had lived like a monk or was gay. Neither was true. He liked women; he was just selective. And he didn't trust anyone.

"Did you have a point? Or are you just calling to annoy me? Because of the two blondes I could choose to deal with, I'd rather Diana over you."

"Oh *Diana*. She is adorable. I'm surprised she's choosing to hang out with you. But as much as I'd love to bust your balls, we gotta go. And lucky for you it's in your neighborhood. Meet me on your north corner in five minutes."

Showtime. "On it."

Rafe turned to Diana. "I need to go out for a minute. Take care of something for Lucia. I'll run by the store on the way home. Do you need anything?"

She shook her head. "That's sweet of you. I'll probably take a walk myself and do a little bit of shopping."

"Okay. I'll see you back here for dinner?" He retrieved the extra house key from the kitchen and brought it to her. "You'll probably get back before I do."

"Maybe not. I need a lot of stuff. I'll probably head out and see if I can find a pair of sandals. I have a little money left from what you gave me the other day. And in case we go back to Noah's or I meet Lucia for lunch or something, I want to have something besides the same pair of sneakers."

He frowned. Why hadn't he thought of that? *Oh yeah, like women's fashion was high on the list of priorities.* Well, except for lingerie. That could be the highest of priorities depending on who was wearing it. "Oh. Sorry, I should have thought about that. I can take you myself if you want."

She shook her head. "Somehow I doubt you want to go shoe shopping. Go. Go do whatever it is you have to do. I'll see you later."

Rafe hated to just leave her behind. But he had work to do. Besides, she said she was fine.

So then why is every instinct telling you she's not?

DIANA WASTED NO TIME.

The moment Rafe left the apartment, dressed in all black and with his *don't fuck with me* face on, she was off the couch and sliding her sneakers on. There was no way she'd be able to follow him on foot. He was too good. She was glad she'd put one of those friend-tracker apps on her phone. Since he'd bought her the phone and they were on the same home network, the app loaded to his phone too.

It was low tech, but it worked.

She was out the door in a flash, keeping an eye on

the direction Rafe was headed. Along the way, she passed a shoe store and stopped. She grabbed the first pair labeled in her size and was out in minutes. Now at least her cover was set.

And just what are you going to say when you find him? Maybe she hadn't thought this through all the way, but no way she was going to miss a chance to get some valuable intel.

Or maybe he's meeting someone... a female someone.

Diana scowled. Theoretically, she shouldn't even care. She didn't want him. *Uh-huh.* It wasn't like he was her boyfriend. And she wasn't stupid enough to think a man who looked like Rafe was a monk. Yesterday there'd been a certain closeness between them. But it wasn't like he'd made a move. He might be off to see someone. She needed to be careful of that before she started to believe the madness.

She checked the app on her phone and cursed. He was moving a lot more quickly than she was. She'd need some assistance if she wanted to keep up. Also, he had the advantage of knowing where they were going and she didn't, which was now glaringly obvious.

"Oh no. Wait!" She held up her hand to signal a man who was getting out of a cab right behind her.

"You need this one?" The man smiled at her in a

vaguely flirty way, but Diana ignored him, pushing past and catapulting into the back seat of the cab.

"Please hurry and make the next left."

"You in some kind of trouble, lady?" The cabbie glanced at her in the rearview mirror, but at least they were moving.

"Not exactly. I'm following my boyfriend. I think he's cheating on me." It was the only thing she could think of, but apparently it wasn't interesting enough for the cabbie to care because he just shrugged and stepped on the gas.

She was able to direct him to the corner where the GPS showed Rafe.

Her cabbie signaled and stopped at the corner up ahead. Diana gave him a twenty-dollar bill and hustled out of the car.

"Thanks!" She glanced around but couldn't see him. What the hell? According to GPS, he should be right— Oh, there he was, ducking down an alley.

She scrambled after him, nearly getting run over in the process. She inched closer to the alley entrance. Then she heard clanging trash bins.

"Fuck off me, man!"

The shout rang down the alley, and Diana instinctively shrank back against the wall. What was that?

There was a stick on the ground near her feet, and

she hurriedly picked it up. It wasn't much, but it was better than nothing. What the hell had she gotten herself into? Belatedly, she realized just how dumb this plan was. She should have at least brought a weapon.

Why yes, let's follow Rafe into an unfamiliar part of the city and then down an alley. Smart girl.

But then there was another shout, one that sounded kind of familiar. Was that Rafe? Diana clutched the wooden stick harder. That sounded like him. By now the low timbre of his voice was something she was getting used to. Her instincts told her to run, but instead she held her ground.

Inching forward toward the sounds of scuffling, she paused right before the corner. She peered around the edge, keeping low to the ground, hoping she wouldn't be seen.

Rafe was on the ground, grappling with some guy. She couldn't even see what he looked like because every time she thought she'd catch a glimpse of his face, he'd move or throw another punch. Diana held a hand over her mouth, not wanting to make a sound and possibly distract him.

Although it didn't look like he needed any help.

Holy hell, the man could move. Diana winced and shrank back again as Rafe and the other man grappled and rolled until they were finally both on their feet. It was like watching a fiercely choreographed dance with kicks and punches flying. The only difference being that someone could end up dead.

The thought was sobering. Because not only could Rafe end up dead, but she could too. How did she know the other man didn't have some friends around who might come along and find her? This was truly not one of her best ideas. She was backing up, thinking she could run back to the main road, when her foot hit a bottle. It went skittering into the alley, the sound ricocheting off the concrete and brick.

Both men glanced over at her. The other guy smirked before turning back around, obviously not judging her as much of a threat.

Rafe, on the other hand, looked gobsmacked. His mouth fell open. "Diana? What the hell are you doing?"

While he was distracted, the other man drew a knife. In that moment, Diana could have sworn her heart stopped. In slow motion, she watched the gleam of sunlight on silver as the long blade was exposed. And she reacted without even thinking.

"No!" She sprang forward and raised the wooden stick in her hands over her head.

The guy heard her, but it was too late for him to react. She brought the stick down with all the strength she had, clubbing him over the head. He swayed, and

Rafe rushed forward and put him in a headlock of some sort. The seconds ticked by, and the guy slowly slumped, landing in a crumpled pile.

Rafe stepped over the body and grabbed her arm. "Come on. We have to get out of here." He wasn't giving her much choice, so even though Diana was still in shock, her feet had to move to keep up with him, otherwise she would have been dragged. Finally she managed to find her voice.

"Who was that?"

Rafe didn't even look at her. "That doesn't matter."

"Doesn't matter? I just killed a guy. Oh my God, I think I just killed somebody."

"I promise all you did was stun him." They'd gotten back to Grand Street, and Rafe held up his hand to hail a cab. One stopped immediately. He fixed her with an intense look. "Don't say anything until we're back at home. Got it?"

She nodded numbly as they climbed into the cab.

He had his phone out in a second and made a call. "You tracking him?"

She couldn't hear the other end of the line, and it was killing her.

"There was a complication, but the muscle he hired is incapacitated." More talking she couldn't hear. He added,

"Not what you think. I need to take Diana home, then I'll come in for debrief." Again silence, before he slid his gaze over her. "Not sure yet, but I'm going to find out."

His dark gaze stripped her bare in the back of the cab. There was a part of her that wished he could see through her. Then he could unmask all the lies and just see her.

Once they arrived outside Rafe's place, he handed over money for the taxi and then tugged her arm. They didn't speak on the elevator ride up either. But as soon as they crossed the threshold, she jumped on the offensive. Better to strike first, right?

"What the hell was that?"

Rafe sighed and leaned on the mantel. "Oskar needed me."

"Oskar? The guy who works for your brother-in-law? Viking-looking dude who flirted with me?"

"Yes, him." He paused for a second and then scowled. "You think he looks like a Viking?"

Diana rolled her eyes. "That's what you're focusing on?"

"He's my partner. Sometimes. Someone we need to get off the street finally showed his face. He took off running and Oskar went after him. I stayed to deal with his muscle." His gaze narrowed a hair. "And then you showed up. I would love to hear the story of how that happened."

Rafe DeMarco was a hard son of a bitch to read. He looked calm. Composed even. There was no tension around his lips. Even his voice was low and soothing.

But her instincts told her she needed to play this as close to the truth as she dared. Her life might depend on it.

She held up her bag. "I was shopping. They didn't have my size at the store on Second Place, so I grabbed a cab and went to the one on West Thames." It was a calculated risk. Bootsman Shoes was on practically every other block. "I was coming out when I saw you turn into that alley. Well, at least I thought it was you. I wasn't sure until I saw you fighting with that guy." She didn't have to fake the trembling in her hands. Adrenaline and fear still coursed through her. "I mean, he had a knife. And I—" Her brain replayed every action she'd taken. The concern that she'd hurt the guy was real. The fear. It was the first time since she'd started this whole thing that she was terrified she was making a mistake. She was playing in a sandbox with actual killers.

"What in the world possessed you to follow me down an alley? Didn't you realize you could have been hurt?"

"Well, excuse me for saving your ass. Next time I'll

let the random thug slice you into sashimi!" He was mad at her for helping him? Asshole. "And what about you? You think traipsing down dark alleys after people who want to hurt you is a good idea?"

"It would have been fine. That was nothing but a workout."

She blinked. "A workout? He had a knife! Seriously, what is wrong with you? Where would you have been if I hadn't come after you?"

He opened his mouth, then snapped it shut and hung his head. A low chuckle escaped and his shoulder shook. "I'm trying to decide if you're reckless or just insane. So far, I'm leaning toward the latter. How this works is while you're here, I take care of you, not the other way around."

She crossed her arms. "Funny. That still doesn't sound like thank you."

Rafe barked a laugh, then scrubbed a hand over his face. "Shit. I'm sorry. And thank you." He reached for her hand. After a pause, Diana accepted it. "There are things in my past that I never talk about. It's as much for your safety as it is for mine. But I need you to just trust that I'm more than qualified to handle an asshole with a knife."

Normally that would have sounded like a line to Diana, but she knew coming from him, it was the complete truth. She squeezed his hand back. "Okay. But I just need you to acknowledge one thing."

"What's that, Diana?"

She secretly thrilled at the way his voice lowered to a near growl when he said her name. Because her vagina would swear she had skin in the game.

"I just need you to acknowledge that I totally saved your life back there."

After a beat, Rafe let out a roar of laughter.

Diana stared. A completely unguarded, laughing Rafe was vajayjay kryptonite. *Wow.* Something pulled deep and low in her abdomen just as her nipples tightened to pebbles.

At her gasp, he sobered quickly. The air changed around them, and Diana shivered. She knew what was coming before he even moved, but there was no bracing for it. He gently tugged her against him, giving her every chance to pull back, but no matter the commands her brain gave, her body refused to comply. *Sorry, brain can't come to the phone right now. She's been body snatched by the libido.*

Rafe slid his arms around her, bringing her body against his. His lips were gentle but demanding. A spike of electricity flared between them, scorching her lips when his tongue dipped in. With a low groan, he shifted their angle, kissing her deeper and ripping a moan from her as her whole body started to melt.

She didn't have the defenses to fight off those long-dormant feelings. Somewhere in the far recesses of her mind, alarm bells rang, starting as a low buzz but quickly intensifying to a sharp clang.

He dragged his lips from hers and stared at her. His muttered curse echoed her own feelings. "We're going to pick this conversation back up. But right now I need to call this incident in to the office."

Diana wished she had something pithy to say, but at the moment her brain was still struggling to rev up and her libido was about ready to cut somebody.

7

Rafe wasn't sure how to dispel the awkwardness that lay between them now, so he went with the old standby. Ignore it.

"I'm just going to make that call and take a shower. You can order some food. If you want, I mean. You'll find a bunch of takeout menus by the phone."

Diana didn't seem any more eager to look him in the eye. "Right. I'll figure it out."

She spun on her heel and went into the kitchen while Rafe continued down the hall to his room. What the hell was wrong with him? You'd think he'd never kissed a woman before. Memories of her lips, warm and firm against his, sent another shot of adrenaline through his veins. He'd never had a woman respond to him the way Diana did. So open and completely uninhibited. His response had been just as incendiary.

After a quick status update with Oskar, Rafe hurried through a shower, inspecting his skin while the water pounded on his back. There was a shallow cut on his inner arm. He hadn't escaped the knife completely it seemed. Considering how shocked he'd been to see Diana standing in that alley, he was lucky he hadn't taken a knife to the heart.

There was something about the woman that got under his skin. An image of her, soft and needy after the kiss, grabbed him by the dick. Jesus. He was harder at just the thought of her than he'd been for any woman he'd had under him. She distracted him. That made him sloppy.

A dangerous thing.

Not to mention the fact that her story about seeing him while out shopping didn't quite add up.

Scowling, he cranked the water all the way to cold. The shock to his system wasn't nearly enough to eradicate all thoughts of her, but it made his erection go down. Slightly.

He toweled off and then walked into his room to find clothes. While he stood in the doorway to the closet, his mind went over the events of the afternoon again and again. She'd shown up in the alley at the worst possible moment, a point in her favor to telling the truth. If she'd been following him all along, he would have noticed.

Not to mention she would have had time to find a good hiding place. Add to that the shock on her face at watching him fight. No one could fake that expression. Diana had been terrified.

But despite things having a rational explanation, something about the situation still didn't sit right with him. With a growl of frustration, he yanked on sweatpants and a T-shirt before leaving his room.

The only way he'd get any real answers was to talk to Diana. Carefully.

Diana stood with her back to him in the kitchen, taking something out of the oven.

"You cooked for me?"

"I can't take credit for it. I found the lasagna in the freezer. But I figured this would be faster than ordering out." Diana rocked on her heels as she spoke.

For the first time in a good long while, Rafe had no idea what to do or say. And for someone who was so used to having all the answers, it was unnerving as hell. Diana had *cooked* for him. How could something so simple twist him up? *Because you like it.* He shoved the thought aside and glanced up at her. She gave him a sheepish smile.

Rafe's gaze drifted back to the lasagna in front of him. His stomach grumbled and his mouth watered. It smelled fucking incredible. She'd made a large salad to go with it and laid out place settings at his small dinette table with napkins neatly folded under the silverware. A small candle burned in the center of the table.

He hadn't even realized he owned a candle.

Rafe approached the table cautiously, the way you might approach a bomb. "You didn't have to go to all this trouble."

She shrugged and gave him another one of her timid smiles. "It's no trouble. Go, sit down. I'll pour you a glass of wine."

Again, Rafe shifted on his feet, unsure of what to do. Other than Nonna, and occasionally his sister, no one had ever taken care of him like this. He had no idea what to do with the kind gesture, and a simple thank-you somehow didn't seem like enough.

As he looked around the room, it hit him that this was the closest he'd been to living with someone in years. Her shoes were next to his, lined up by the front door. The lap blanket she'd used earlier while watching television was thrown haphazardly over the end of the couch in the living room.

The fruit his housekeeper had purchased was now arranged in a clear glass bowl on the center of the kitchen island. When was the last time he'd had fruit on display? *Uh, try never.* The thought made him smile.

Slowly, she was doing things to make his apartment

seem like home. More than he'd ever done. Hell, he'd never even had anyone over. And he'd been here for a year. How fucked up was that?

"Seriously, Diana, this is great. But you didn't have to do this."

She brought over a plate with salad already served out. "I figure you can serve the lasagna yourself. I can never plate it well."

He laughed. "I got it. You go ahead and pour the wine."

Her smile slid a little when their fingertips grazed. He saw a flash of heat. Or was that panic? He was unsure. Either way, he served them both. She brought over the wine, putting the larger glass in front of him.

When she sat, her smile was tighter, but she said, "Go on, eat." She started in on her salad with gusto, and he followed suit. When she took a large gulp of wine, he watched the way her tongue peeked out to lick her bottom lip before sipping, and he had to bite back a curse.

What are you doing here? He wasn't used to feeling unsure.

The whole thing was just a mess. He'd never had problems with women. *Probably because those encounters were just sex*. But he liked Diana. He sort of felt responsible for her, though he had no right to those feelings. She wasn't his.

He'd found her last Friday night. And she didn't seem any closer to getting her affairs in order. He knew she'd called for her cards, but that always took a while. So for the time being, he *was* responsible for her, and he didn't want to take advantage of that.

Those truths still didn't stop him from wanting to taste her lips again. He wanted to know if he had imagined that flash of heat, the connection. And of course, his dick, persistent as it was, wanted to know if the promise of heat could deliver.

He took a bite of his lasagna, the garlic and tomato hitting his tongue with the perfect blend. He moaned. "I forgot how good Anna's lasagna is. Do not tell Nonna, but I think this is almost as good as hers."

She took another large gulp of wine even as she laughed. "I won't tell. I still owe you one for the whole saving-my-life deal. Thank you for that, by the way. I'm not sure if that point made it across since I was too busy being a brat that day. Although I suppose we're even now after I took out that guy in the alley for you."

He shook his head. "We're not even because I'm not keeping score. And you don't have to say thank you. It's no big deal."

She gave him a pointed look. "You mean you rappel

down the side of a cliff to rescue damsels in distress every day? And here I thought I was special."

He laughed. "Yes, that's in my superhero description. You were the third one that week. Granted, you were also probably the mouthiest."

She laughed. "I am not mouthy. How was I supposed to know you do things like that all the time? I mean, what is rappelling anyway?"

His lips twitched. "It's a legitimate sport." Better she think he was some crazy adrenaline junkie than guess the truth.

She lifted her glass of wine and he followed suit, but once again he got distracted watching her mouth. Fuck, if he didn't address that kiss, he was going to drive himself insane. He put his glass back down and watched her for a moment.

They ate in companionable silence for a while, and finally he figured the hell with it. "So, can we talk about that kiss?"

A deep pink flush tinted her cheeks, and he had to resist the urge to reach over and caress a thumb over what looked like the softest skin he'd ever seen.

She lifted her lashes and met his gaze. "You mean when you kissed me?"

Rafe almost choked on his salad. "I kissed *you*? I

seem to recall you standing on your tiptoes and leaning into me."

She laughed. "So you're suggesting that I totally made the first move?"

"Yes." He grinned. "Clearly you did. It's okay. I know I'm irresistible."

She laughed so hard she snorted a little. Holy hell, why was that sexy? *It's sexy because you're horny*. That was it. Nothing more. At least he knew he wasn't the only one affected. Diana was downing her wine fairly quickly. Was she nervous?

"You really are full of yourself, aren't you?" She stood and went to the counter, then brought back the bottle of wine she'd already opened to let breathe. She poured them both a glass before taking her seat again.

Rafe frowned. "So you *don't* think I'm sexy?" She coughed as her face flamed again, and he grinned. "I'll save you from answering that. Of course I am. How can I not be?"

"And so modest too."

He shrugged. "We all know our strengths. But seriously—" He cleared his throat. "I didn't mean to take advantage of the situation. You know you're safe here. I would never—"

Her eyes went wide and she immediately shook her head. "No. I didn't think— That wasn't what I thought at all. It just"—she licked her lips again, and Rafe had to bite his to keep from groaning—"happened."

He nodded, just on the verge of telling her that if she kept doing that lip thing, it was going to happen again. But they had other things to discuss. He needed to know more about her. Anything. So far all he knew was the surface stuff, and he wanted to go deeper. But given what she'd already been through, he wanted her to give him that information willingly. He didn't want to have to go digging for it.

"So I know you said you didn't want to call anyone before, but you must have friends or family who are worried about you."

Diana finished her last sip of wine and immediately poured another glass.

She shook her head. "I do have one friend, but she has a family. Little ones. I'd have to explain my bruises and my situation. So it's basically like I have no one."

He nodded. "You know, I find that even when people think they have no one, there's at least one person they can call. I don't like the idea of you being all alone. Not with that asshole still out there."

She swallowed hard. Her gaze shifting to her plate, she picked at the rest of her salad. "I'm fine. I left. Right now he doesn't know where I am. So maybe that's for the best. If he tries to check my phone or something, it's down at the bottom of the ravine. There's no way he can find me."

Rafe watched her closely. His questioning was making her edgy.

"Diana, you can trust me. I can help you. Tell me his name. I have friends in law enforcement. They could pay him a visit. I'll attest to the bruising that I saw on your body. Guys like that shouldn't be allowed to walk the earth. No one should ever put their hands on you." He scowled. "He should pay for that."

The ferocity of his anger surprised even him. And her gaze fluttered up to meet his.

She parted her lips as if to say something, and then she shook her head. "I don't want to talk about him. I just want to relax. Drink some wine."

Rafe glanced at his glass, the maroon liquid still untouched. He paused and then looked closer. There was a bit of residue on the rim. Was that... no. His heart protested even as his mind and more importantly his training blared a warning.

"You know, I never did ask what you got while you were shopping."

Diana paused with her glass halfway to her mouth. Rafe caught a glimpse of something—maybe panic—in her eyes. Then she shook her head.

"Shoes. Remember, I told you when we got back. I

got some sandals so I'd have something nicer to wear in case we went to see your friends again. I felt out of place so dressed down last time." But her smile didn't quite reach her eyes. "They're in the living room. Want to see?"

He shook his head. "After dinner."

Diana fidgeted with her napkin, smoothing it out and then replacing it under her silverware. He noticed that her eyes kept going back to his glass.

What was she waiting for, exactly? Rafe was pretty damn sure he knew. Although he couldn't think of a single reason Diana might want to hurt him.

Let's just make this easier on everyone, he thought.

He took the smallest bite of salad and then reached for the wineglass, knocking his fingers against the stem roughly.

"Oh no!" Diana jumped up as the red liquid spread across the surface of the glass table.

She should have been upset that her plan had just been ruined, but truthfully all she felt was... relief.

"It's okay. I'll get a towel." She could feel Rafe's eyes on her as she rushed into the kitchen.

The dish towels were in a drawer on the island, and

as she grabbed one, Diana took the time to calm herself. Yes, her plan to get him talking had just been ruined, but that didn't explain why she felt so relieved. Was she getting attached to him? And why was she feeling guilty? The man was a killer, and she had only planned to ask him questions...well to tie him up, ask him questions and search his place . She wouldn't have hurt him. She wasn't like him; she didn't harm people even when they deserved it.

"Are you okay?" Rafe's voice over her shoulder startled her slightly. "I should have asked that earlier. That was intense, and you have every right to be upset right now."

Diana turned so that he wasn't at her back anymore. Having him so close was unnerving. "I am. A little. But I just did what I had to do. I'm trying to remember that. Besides, he would have killed me if he'd had the chance."

She walked back to the table, aware of Rafe following her. He took his seat and just watched her with those eyes that seemed to see everything.

"You're right, he would have killed you. Then it would have been even worse for him. Because if he'd touched even one hair on your head, I would have killed him. Oskar checked on him after I called the incident in. He's fine. He's in the hospital. A tourist saw him knocked out and called for an ambulance after we left."

Warmth burst through Diana's chest at his rough declaration. Their eyes met and held. In that moment, she had no doubt he meant what he said. And she had a feeling if he ever got his hands on her imaginary ex, there might be some blood spilled.

No one had ever stood up for her before. Sure, growing up her father had been indulgent, but he'd always been too busy for her. And her memories of her mother were hazy. She just remembered her mother as smiling and loving. And certainly her brothers had never been protective. For the most part, they'd been either disdainful or just ignored her.

But somehow a perfect stranger had made her feel like she would never be alone again if she didn't choose to be. She needed to get her mind around that.

More like get your mind around the fact that you have Stockholm Syndrome! You shouldn't feel this way for a man you know is a killer!

Diana ignored the screaming sound of her common sense trying to catch her attention. Every time Rafe had raised his glass, she'd held her breath, torn between anticipation and guilt. She hadn't been sure whether she wanted him to drink the drugged wine or not. Maybe it was the sincerity in his eyes, the way he looked at her when he told her she could trust him. But she wanted to trust him. Wanted to believe that the connection she felt was real.

You are a traitor.

There was an internal war waging in her brain. There was the part of her that needed to know the truth. But was this the way to get it?

And then there was that part of her that was a woman. The part of her that wanted to believe the sincerity she saw in his gaze. The part that melted at how protective he was of her. The man had leaped into a ravine to save her. He'd invited her into his home because she had nowhere else to go. And she knew that if anyone ever tried to hurt her, Rafe would stop them.

"I wouldn't want you to do that," she finally whispered.

He leaned forward so she couldn't avoid his eyes. "You may not want it, but I wouldn't be able to stop it. You do something to me, Diana, trigger something in me that I can't control. Any man who hurts you might as well have a signed death warrant on file because he doesn't deserve to breathe the same air you do. I wish you would tell me the name of the man who did that to you." He inclined his chin toward her ribs.

Despite how violent his words were, something inside her responded like he'd just offered her flowers and chocolate instead of her imaginary ex's head on a platter. Why was his insistence on protecting her so insanely sexy? There was something she found in his eyes, a mixture of longing and need and concern. He wasn't like any man she'd ever known.

"You don't have to protect me. I haven't met many guys who want to do that," she finally said, and she was no longer playing a role. Truthfully, she hadn't come across any men who wanted to treat their girlfriends the way Rafe described. Unless you counted the heroes in the romance novels she devoured.

"You hadn't met me yet," he growled. "You deserve everything, Diana. To be protected and cherished every single day." His voice lowered. "Then debauched thoroughly every night."

And ladies and gentleman, just like that her panties were toast, incinerated by the blazing heat generated between them.

"Oh my God," she stammered, completely taken off guard by his raw, blatantly unapologetic statement.

Why did it have to be this guy to awake the sleeping libido monster inside her? Why did she feel this way with him? Why not any other guy?

None of that mattered to her in this moment. Because every instinct in her body told her that she could trust this man. Every instinct told her that this was what she needed to do. That she had to touch him.

So for once in her life, she didn't overanalyze or plan out a detailed scheme to accomplish her goal. She followed her instinct.

His eyes registered only the briefest surprise as she sat in his lap and curled her hand around his neck.

Holy hell, could the man kiss. The first brush of his lips was gentle, just a whisper of movement. He pulled back briefly, his eyes fluttering open so he could assess her.

She held her breath and prayed for more. When his lips returned to hers, she could barely hide her moan of relief.

The next kiss had more weight, his lips sliding over hers, warming her entire body with just that easy contact. And then his tongue peeked out and moved against her lips, and she gasped.

Rafe took full advantage of that small sound from her open mouth and slid his tongue inside to explore.

Diana melted into the kiss, meeting each thrust of his tongue with hers, relishing the way he dug his hands into her hair at the nape of her neck, gently tugging, angling her so he could kiss her deeper.

Her skin felt too tight, her breath too shallow, and something low in her core pulled tight. With every lick of Rafe's tongue and every tug of his hand, she molded herself against him, pressing her breasts into his side.

Rafe growled low and shifted her on his lap so she straddled him. *Oh. My. God.* That felt so damn good, the pulsing length of him directly where she needed it so badly. Where she longed to have him.

He tore his lips from hers and muttered a low, unintelligible curse before dragging his lips back to hers and kissing her again. Diana wanted more. So much more.

And she knew Rafe could give it to her.

8

Control gone.

Never mind that this might be a bad idea. Never mind that his instincts were still searching for a reason not to trust her. He wanted her. For once he wanted softness and hope. He'd lived in the dark for too long. He didn't want to be that person anymore.

He wasn't in that world anymore. He lived in the light now. He'd thought like a killer for too damn long. Rafe stood with her in his arms. He wasn't sure where he was taking them, but he needed a good surface to spread her out on. She had so many enticing dips and curves, and he wanted to explore them all.

Lifting her easily, he carried her to his bedroom and placed her gently in the middle of the bed. Diana spread her arms out to stabilize herself and then giggled as he crawled over her.

"I feel like a gazelle being stalked by a lion." She spread her legs to make room for him.

Rafe settled against her, feeling her heat even through the thick material of her jeans. Which reminded him that they were both overdressed. He tugged the denim down her legs, leaving her in a pair of plain white cotton panties. Why the fuck was that so hot? He made quick work of his own clothes, tossing everything in a pile at the foot of the bed. Diana's eyes widened when she took him in, and Rafe was never more grateful for the punishing workout regime he maintained. Being a professional bad guy had taken its toll on his psyche, but it had done insane things for his muscle definition.

"Wow," Diana breathed. "You look like you were carved out of concrete." Her eyes roamed over every inch of him, finally landing on the huge erection that he didn't even bother trying to hide from her.

"Yeah, that part too, huh?"

A blush stole up her neck and cheeks. "Definitely that part."

He crawled over her, kissing up her right leg until he got to the edge of those fucking sexy-ass panties. It made him think of when he'd had to talk his way into a girl's panties in high school. So innocent and fucking sweet. All the reasons Diana could do so much better than a guy like him.

"I wish I could be better for you," he said before he thought about it. But he'd taken this as slow as he could, had given her time to turn him down, but he wasn't giving her any more.

He wasn't that fucking nice.

"You are exactly who you're supposed to be, Rafael DeMarco. And I like that."

He might not be the good guy she deserved, but he was the guy who could fuck her like she needed. He could worship her perfect body so she'd never again accept anything less than adoration from any man in the future.

He tugged the panties down and then instantly replaced the fabric with his tongue. Surprised, Diana arched into his touch. Soft moans floated down to him as he grasped her under the hips and pulled her closer. He needed to get deeper. When he finally thrust his tongue in and then pulled back to focus on her clit, she screamed as she shook and clenched against his face.

The reaction just spurred him on, and he didn't let her rest or pull back. He swirled his tongue around the little hot button that he knew would take her there again. Rafe loved everything about being with her this way, having her honey all over his face and feeling her come unraveled with each suck, lick, and touch.

"Rafe, you have to stop. I-I can't take any more!"

He shook his head and she squealed when the movement brushed his tongue back and forth over the lips of her sex.

Oh, you like that, do you?

He did it again, deliberately, tickling the plump lips around her sex with delicate licks and kisses before he thrust a finger inside her. She broke again, crying out and grabbing his hair so hard he was sure he'd lost a few strands.

Totally worth the sacrifice, he thought when he looked up a few minutes later to see a look of complete and total satisfaction on her face. She looked dazed.

He wiped his mouth gently on her inner thigh and then placed a soft kiss on her belly. Her being dazed and softened from pleasure was exactly what he wanted. He knew he was big, and given the way her slick flesh had clamped around his finger, she was going to be a tight fit.

He rolled away briefly to grab the box of condoms that had been unopened since he moved here nearly a year ago. *What does that say about normal life?* Well, he had a lot of making up to do. Hands trembling with need, he quickly sheathed himself, then repositioned himself between her thighs.

When he slid inside, her eyes flew open and her fingers curled into his shoulders. She was so wet he'd gone farther than he meant to, and Rafe had to bite the inside of his cheek to maintain control. There was nothing like this, being held in her soft, wet heat.

"Oh!" Diana's wide eyes locked on his.

He stopped, giving her time to adjust. She shuddered and her pussy clamped around him so hard his eyes almost rolled into the back of his head.

"Goddamn, you are so damn tight."

He couldn't take it anymore. He pulled back and then slid forward all the way. Her muscles sucked him in and rippled around his dick as he thrust harder and harder. *Slow down, don't hurt her, take your time.* His brain screamed at him to be careful with her, but all his good intentions were lost when her hands slid over his shoulders and down his back to land on his ass. Her nails curled into the flexing muscles.

"It feels so good—don't stop." Diana sobbed against his shoulder when she came again, and the tight, clamping rhythm of her release pushed him right to the edge.

"Fuck! Your pussy was made for me, you know that?"

He growled it right in her ear, noting how she got even wetter at the dirty words.

"Rafe!"

Her scream was the last thing he heard before he was sucked under in a whirling storm that fractured everything into brilliant white lights.

HOLY HELL, what had she just done?

Her inner sex kitten stretched languorously. *You had yourself a whole bunch of orgasms.*

She'd meant to fuck with his life, but she hadn't meant to actually fuck him. Jesus H. Christ. She was so screwed.

Ain't that the truth.

The man had stamina, that much was not in question. Diana huffed out a breath and pushed her hair out of her face. Next to her, Rafe lay sprawled over the other side of the bed, looking just as destroyed as she felt. They'd been at it for hours, and it was only now that he was allowing her to rest.

He wasn't really allowing her to rest; it was more like he'd had to take a break too. She didn't have much experience, but he'd demanded that she give as good as she got. And if the dopey, satisfied look on his face was any indication, she'd done that. Yeah, but at what cost? Unwanted guilt wormed its way into her heart and planted a seed.

So. Screwed.

This whole plan hinged on her being as cold and calculating as he was. *But that's not the truth, is it?* She'd made a mistake at the party. Hell, before the party. She'd started to see him as a person. Not just a man, but someone like her who'd made bad decisions along the way. She'd humanized him, and there was no coming back from that. She'd have to live with the guilt.

When he turned his head and saw her watching him, his lips stretched into a lazy smile. Then, in a sudden motion that made Diana squeak, his arm wrapped around her middle and dragged her right up next to him. His face nuzzled into the curve of her neck, and she had to fight back a sigh of contentedness. Who would have thought Rafe would be a snuggler?

"Do you need anything? Thirsty?"

Diana shook her head. "I don't think I could move if the building was on fire. My legs are jelly."

His low, sexy laugh sent chills up and down her spine, and her traitorous nipples immediately stood at attention. She scowled. After a marathon session like they'd just had, every part of her should be satisfied. But no, apparently certain parts of her would always react to

Rafe even when she felt like she'd been wrung completely dry.

"Good. That means my work here is done." Rafe kissed her behind the ear and then stretched. "I'm going to shave and then take a shower. You should rest."

Diana watched as he got out of the bed and walked over to the dresser. She didn't bother to hide the fact that she was staring. A naked Rafe was truly a sight to behold. With his dark, ebony hair and that honey skin tone, he looked like the perfect fantasy of *tall, dark, and handsome*. That description would forever be modified to *tall, dark, insanely muscular, and handsome* for Diana. She couldn't keep the smile off her face when he bent over to get something out of the dresser.

Stupid vagina.

Everything on him, including the incredible ass currently in front of her, was tight, firm, and looked like you could bounce quarters off it.

He turned around and noticed her staring. "Keep looking at me like that and you're going to get fucked... again. Is that what you want?"

The low timbre of his voice made her wet. Just like that. So simple. So easy. "Jesus. You're a machine, and I'm sore all over. I think I need a rest."

He prowled back to the bed, leaning over to trail kisses up her leg. "Wish I could say I'm sorry. But I'm not. And if you're sore, there are a few other places I didn't touch, kiss, or fuck last night." His gaze flickered to hers and he winked.

Oh fuck.

Her inner sex kitten: Yes. Hell yes. Get the lube. ALL the lube.

Her: Gulp.

Her mouth hung open and he chuckled to himself. "Keep that up and you'll catch my dick in your mouth."

Diana just laughed and pulled the covers over her head. She heard the bathroom door shut a few seconds later.

She blushed and pulled the sheet around her body. The sounds of the shower filtered in from behind the door across from the bed. How he had the energy to even stand upright, she would never know. It felt like every bone in her body had been turned into jelly. *Good sex will do that to you.* At least that was what she'd heard.

Damn, I can't believe that's what I've been missing all this time.

Nope. Uh-uh. She wasn't going to reflect on his talented mouth, fingers, or dick right now. She was at DEFCON 1. She'd slept with him. She needed to regroup. Get her priorities in order. She could still do this.

Are you sure you want to?

Tears pricked her lids. This was so fucked. What did she have if she didn't have this? She'd made a mistake, and now she needed to live with it. She couldn't dwell on how disappointed she was with herself. Or how much she was betraying her family.

The sound of her phone ringing pulled her out of her thoughts. With the sheet wrapped around her, she ran out to the living room to get her phone from her jacket. By the time she got there, it had stopped ringing.

Charisse. She immediately called her back.

"Hey honey, you okay? You didn't check in last night like usual."

That's because she'd been busy hanging on to Rafe's shoulders and trying not to die from too many orgasms. Diana winced. Constant phone calls would have been suspicious, but she'd been keeping Charisse updated each day with a quick text message. Her friend was already worried enough about her going through with this crazy plan.

"I— Uh, I'm sorry. I didn't mean to make you worry."

"Well, I did worry. Where the hell were you? Please don't tell me if it was anything dangerous."

"No. Not dangerous. I just... fell asleep."

Charisse was silent for a beat. Then two. "Oh. My. God. You slept with him!"

"It's not my fault. But he kissed me... and..." Her

voice trailed. "Well, I don't really know what happened after that. I know I shouldn't have, okay? I feel shitty about it."

Charisse stayed silent.

"Fuck. Say something."

"Was it good?"

Was it ever. "Seriously, I tell you I fucked the enemy and you ask if it was good?"

"I mean, was it?"

"Yes, damn it."

"But you still want to go through with the plan."

"I don't really have a choice. That's why I'm here."

"Or maybe you do have a choice, and you've lived with this for so long and ignored who you are as a person and as a woman and you needed this. Maybe it's time to bury this vendetta."

"What, and live a blissfully shagged life with my father's killer?"

"When you put it that way, it does sound a little warped." Charisse took a breath. "So what's the plan, Stan? You going to sleep with him again?"

Vagina: Fuck yes.

Brain: Hell no.

Her brain won out despite the deep pull in her belly. "No. I'm going to do my best to wrap this up and stay alive."

She glanced around the kitchen where the remains of their dinner were still on the table, spilled wine and all. The place was a damn disaster. The situation just kept spinning more and more out of control, and she was afraid that eventually she'd be thrown off the ride. She blew out a breath as she grabbed a dishrag and started cleaning. It was something to take her mind off how crazy the situation was at least. She'd made such a mess of things. So it was time to get to plan B, or she was going to make a deadly mistake.

"I just—"

"What, Char?"

"I just hope you know what you're doing."

"Me too. I always have the Corbin James contingency." Corbin James was the fictitious ex she'd created for herself. If things got too hot, she'd leave some clues that her ex had found her, and she'd vanish. Rafe would be so busy looking for a ghost that it would be too late by the time he found her real trail.

At least she hoped that's how things would go.

"I hope it doesn't come down to that."

"Yeah, me too." Diana put the last of the dishes in the dishwasher and then went back to wipe down the table. She could hear Charisse breathing softly and figured her friend was trying to come up with something to say. But in the end she just sighed.

"Be safe, Diana. Love you."

"Love you too. I'll call you later today when it's safer."

"Uh-huh. Be careful."

"Always."

Diana hung up with a sinking feeling in her stomach. Then she turned, and her stomach dropped completely when she saw Rafe standing in the doorway to the kitchen, watching her with shrewd eyes.

Oh shit! "Hey, there you are. I didn't hear the shower stop." Diana cursed herself silently as soon as she said it. She didn't need to point out to him that she'd been listening for when he was done.

"I finished and came looking for you. I thought you'd be back asleep." He looked over at the clean table. "Apparently I didn't tire you out as well as I thought I did."

Diana blushed. "You did. I only got up because I heard my phone ringing. I figured the least I could do was start cleaning up."

He moved closer. "You don't need to do that. I can think of much better uses for all this extra energy."

Relieved that he was in a playful mood, Diana put her arms around his waist. He hadn't bothered to put a shirt on after his shower, so he was only wearing a pair of loose gym shorts. The scruff that looked so sexy on him was gone now, and he was clean-shaven. It was ridiculous that a man could look so good both ways.

"I've never seen you without the beard. You look good. But I definitely like the stubble too."

"Yeah. I do too. But I noticed the beard marks on your neck. And having the scruff makes it harder for me to do this." He easily picked her up, then covered her lips with his. By the time he pulled back, Diana was dazed and panting.

"So, who was on the phone?" he asked, all while kissing lightly all over her face.

Diana could barely think, and he wanted to ask her questions. She struggled to remember who had called. Then she remembered that she couldn't tell him who had called. No way she was putting Charisse in harm's way.

"I was just checking my messages. I took your advice and texted my friend. She called earlier. I missed it because we were a little occupied."

"Did she leave one?"

"Leave what?" He was using his tongue on the shell of her ear, and it made it hard to think.

He nipped her softly before saying, "A message."

Diana looked up into his eyes and stilled. He knew something. Rafe was watching her a little too closely, and there was something in his eyes that warned her to be careful what she said. Because he would be looking for holes in her story.

"No. She'll probably call back."

She tried to get down, but he held her in position. The sheet had precariously slipped since he'd picked her up, and she could feel the tip of his dick poking up over the top of his shorts.

His gaze was serious even as his voice was feather soft. "Diana?"

Shit, he was going to call her on her lies. She was toast. "Yeah?"

"I think I'm going to need another shower."

Her eyes went wide when he rocked his hips and she could feel the outline of his cock. Yes, she'd just said this was not happening again. Yes, she'd never intended to sleep with him in the first place. Yes, this was a dangerous game she was playing.

She could lie to Charisse all she wanted, but lying to herself was a habit she couldn't abide. She wanted him. Even if that made her hate herself. It was getting nearly impossible to keep track of the lies and who she was supposed to be and when.

Especially when all she really wanted to be with Rafe was herself.

"We could shower together. You know... conserve water."

He nodded slowly. "Environmentally minded. I like that. And I'm down. But first I'm going to make you scream like this. Then I'm going to show you just a few of the things we missed out on last night in my haste to come inside you."

He deliberately rocked against her clit again and he'd called it, all right. She did scream.

9

D*iana was lying to him.*

Rafe knew it in his bones. And he was the idiot who'd slept with her.

He was supposed to be the guy who could walk away. He was supposed to be the guy who wasn't affected by any of this shit. But just the knowledge that he'd gotten it wrong twisted him up inside.

Give her a chance. There might be a reason for the lie. Because no doubt about it. She had been lying about checking her messages the morning he'd caught her in the kitchen. He hadn't called her on it then. Because hell, he was a spy. He knew enough to keep his cards close to his vest until he was ready.

And with her naked in your bed, will you ever be ready?

Several days had passed since he'd crossed that line with her. And he kept trying to pin down the clues.

Figure out what she was hiding. He wanted to be wrong. *Prayed* he was wrong.

The previous day when he'd left for the office, she had kissed him sweetly and told him she'd see him later. Her credit cards had arrived that morning, but neither one of them had uttered a single word about what that meant or about where this was going. When he'd gotten home, they'd continued in that vein, eating dinner together, neither addressing the elephant in the room. Diana didn't seem inclined to confide in him either, Rafe thought grumpily.

When he'd asked her what was on her mind last night, he'd hoped it would at least start the conversation about what her plans were going forward. But she'd distracted him with kisses. *You let yourself be distracted.*

It burned a hole in Rafe's chest that he really didn't know much about her at all. Except her name. That was it. *If you were smart, you would have done a background check.* He shoved that thought aside. *Woulda, shoulda, coulda.*

Before he'd slept with her, she was just a woman he was helping. There was nothing she could gain access to in his apartment. His safe was national-security tight. Sure, she had access to his security panel, but that was just for the house. She was welcome to anything in there that she could carry. And if she tried to make off with the Decker, she'd get a nasty surprise. The thing was booby-trapped.

He didn't use the same password for anything. Both his computer and his safe would require hacker-level decryption equipment.

So he'd had no need to worry about exactly who she was or finding out all the dirty details about her life. *Until now.*

Next to him, Diana slumbered, completely unaware of the direction of his thoughts. It made him feel like a pussy, but he couldn't deny himself the privilege of watching her when she was so vulnerable.

It felt ridiculous that he wasn't sure how to talk to a woman, but he honestly hadn't had much practice in these types of situations. From his covert work, he was used to using... other methods when he needed information from someone.

It turned out that proving you were trustworthy so people voluntarily told you things was an entirely different game.

Finally she moaned and rolled toward him, pillowing her hands under her cheek. Her lashes fluttered against her cheeks gently before her eyes opened. When she saw him watching her, her eyes lit up with pleasure. It did something to him to see her unfiltered reaction. She wasn't even fully awake yet, so there was no artifice or calculation behind her reaction. Just happiness. She was genuinely happy to see him.

"Good morning," he said softly.

"Morning."

She moved closer and burrowed into the crook of his arm. He pulled her near, savoring the warmth and comfort of having someone with him. Due to the dangers of his job, he'd never allowed anyone to get close, so he'd missed this kind of easy intimacy. It wasn't as difficult as he'd thought it would be. Somehow being with Diana felt like the most natural thing in the world.

The sound of her stomach rumbling broke the quiet in the room. Diana's giggles made him smile.

"Hungry, sweetheart?"

She finally pulled her face out of his arm. "Sorry. I'm not sure why, but I'm starving."

Rafe pressed a gentle kiss on her forehead. "That's my cue. I'll see what I can rustle up. Especially since you've been doing such a good job of taking care of me when it should be the other way around. Don't want you to think I don't take care of my guests."

Her eyes lost some of their sparkle and her lips pulled down at the corners slightly. "Right. I'm just going to jump in the shower."

Rafe made a decision. He needed to call Noah for advice. That wasn't a decision he made lightly. This was the man he'd once mentored and thought of as a little brother. A man he'd trained to be a killer and who was now married to his little sister. Who'd knocked up his little sister. Rafe shuddered. That shit was still taking some getting used to.

Once Diana was in the shower and he didn't have to worry about her overhearing, Rafe took his phone out to the living room.

When Noah answered, he sounded distracted. Which quickly changed when he realized who it was. Good to know he still commanded some respect.

Then he said, "You sound like shit. Who kicked your dog?"

So much for respect.

"I had a sleepless night. Fuck off."

Noah laughed. "Hmm. Is that code for sex all night? If so, good for you. Diana seemed cool."

"We are not talking about this," Rafe gritted out.

"Okay, okay. I won't ask you any more questions about the pretty blonde you brought to a family gathering who seems to have you on edge right now. I won't say a damn word. But, on the off chance you *did* want to talk about it, I've been there. There was a time your sister had me all twisted and turned around. It was fucking hell."

The last thing Rafe wanted to hear about was Noah

and his sister. "This is an entirely different situation. Diana and I are... we're not permanent."

"Why not? You think she might be headed back to her family? Or where she's from? Where is she from anyway?"

Rafe rubbed at the back of his neck. He knew what Noah was doing. Nosy as he was, he wasn't just going to let it go. And then, no doubt, Lucia would join in, peppering him with questions until Rafe finally relented and gave in from the exhaustion.

With a sigh, Rafe said, "I think I need to use your boy Matthias."

Silence, then Noah said, "Something not adding up?"

"I heard the end of a conversation a few days ago. I'm not sure exactly what I heard. So I'm trying to figure it out."

"She had the look of someone running from something. Does she need to be saved from herself?"

"I don't know yet. She has some asshole ex. He's the one she's running from. He also kicked her and almost broke her ribs."

Noah's voice went low and deadly. "You want Blake Security to have a *conversation* with him?"

While many of Noah's clients were upper-class businesspeople, he also did pro bono work. People who needed Noah's help getting rid of boyfriends and stalkers. The dregs of society. People the police couldn't or wouldn't help. And maybe Diana would've needed someone like Noah. Except she had *him*.

And if Diana wasn't going to open up on her own, then Rafe would just have to help her along. "I just want to have a look into her past and at that asshole who's still after her. I need to be able to protect her."

"Holy shit, this isn't just some random girl. You're into her."

"She's running from something. I'm trying to help her. That's all."

Noah laughed. "If you think you'll get away with that, you're delusional. It's written all over you. Protectiveness, the desire to kill whoever it was who hurt her. You're staking a claim on her. Oskar said you got cagey when he flirted with her. But I didn't believe him."

"Mind your own business. She just needs help. That's all."

"Uh-huh. Whatever you say, man. I'm just saying it's not like you to not do a thorough vetting first."

Fuck. He already knew that. "I don't know what the fuck happened. I was supposed to just be helping her. Next thing, she's under my skin, you know? With that sassy mouth and all the crazy shit she's doing to my house. There was a candle burning on the table while we ate dinner the other night. A fucking candle, for the love of Christ."

Noah laughed. "This is awesome. I honestly never thought I'd see it. I mean, it's not like I thought you were a monk but hearing you all confused... It's fucking fantastic."

"Fuck you. You going to lend me Matthias or what?"

"*Mi* hacker *es su* hacker."

Rafe rolled his eyes. "Yeah, whatever, man. You know I can do it myself if you're going to give me grief."

"Sure, you can do it yourself. But we both know Matthias will be faster, and you want to spend all your free time with little Miss Hot Blonde. Have to say man, you have excellent taste. She's beautiful. And funny. Lucia loved her. Maybe she'll finally get a sister out of you."

"Don't be a douchebag."

Noah chuckled again. "I'm not exactly sure how to be any other way. Besides, I just want you to have what I found with Lucia. After the things we've done, to have someone look at you like that. I can't even explain it. It gives your life meaning."

Rafe swallowed against a swell of panic unlike anything he'd ever experienced. All his life he'd worked to protect his family, done unspeakable things, all with the aim of making sure they were safe. But he didn't know how to be there for them anymore. He'd had to turn off that part of himself, the part that had once tucked Lucia into bed and read her bedtime stories. He didn't know how to open the floodgates to all that emotion again without drowning in it.

He didn't know how to be the kind of man Diana needed. Deserved. How did a man get that comfortable with putting himself out there? The way they'd been taught, feelings were a weakness. How had Noah gotten around that to open himself up to Lucia? How did he deal with keeping his darkness at bay so he wouldn't hurt the woman he loved?

How did a man who'd been taught to assume the worst learn to trust?

"Rafe, you still there?"

"Yeah, I'm here. I still can't believe my kid sister is married with a baby of her own."

"I know." But Noah sounded proud instead of terrified. It had been quite a revelation to see the changes in him from being with Lucia. Rafe wouldn't have thought there would ever come a day that he'd feel like he could learn something from Noah, but here it was.

"Has Lucia ever lied to you?"

Noah snorted and barked out a laugh. "Man, you don't even want to know some of the things your sister has done. She's a manipulative little thing when she wants to be."

Now it was Rafe's turn to snort. "Lucia? No way. She's always been an angel," he muttered sarcastically.

His sister had been raised to be the good girl. But somewhere along the line, she'd bucked that and started standing on her own. And sometimes that came with deception.

Like the time she and JJ had locked Delaney in the panic room so they could go after a killer.

Shit. He still lost sleep over that one.

He'd watched her grow up and been a surrogate father to her after their parents died. He'd always thought he knew her inside and out. But she had changed in all the time he'd been gone.

"You know as well as I do that your sister is no angel anymore. This is the girl who ditched her security by dressing one of the girls in her office in her clothes so she and JJ could hit a club."

"Oh yeah, that night when I tried to get her back. You should have done something about that."

"Like I could stop her. Have you ever tried to get between Lucia and something she wants? Not if you want to keep your balls."

Rafe chuckled. He had to admit that despite being such a good kid, Lucia was really good at getting her way. She could just turn those big gray eyes on you and you'd cave and give her whatever she wanted. But not like this. She'd always been more... persuasive than sneaky. Nothing like he was seeing with Diana.

"You're right. She could be a handful when she wanted. I blame JJ."

Noah barked a laugh. "You know what, I'm inclined to believe that, but I think sometimes JJ just gives her permission to do things she always wanted to. She sent me a strippergram here at the office when she was pissed at me one time."

"Wait, what? Lucia sent strippers? Why didn't I know this?" Rafe wasn't sure he wanted to continue the conversation. There were certain things he just didn't want to know about his sister.

Noah's laughter carried through the phone, and Rafe couldn't help smiling too. Although it did make him a little sad, as it always did when he was reminded just how long he'd been gone, just how much his time with ORUS had really cost him.

"I don't think I need to know too much about my sister as an adult. I'll just keep thinking of her as a little pip-squeak with pigtails."

Noah's laughter finally trailed off. "That's probably best. But in short, the answer to your question is yes. Lucia has lied to me before. Sometimes when it's minor, and sometimes when it can get her killed. But it's always because she feels like she's doing the right thing."

Rafe suddenly wasn't sure he wanted to borrow Matthias anymore. What the hell was he doing assuming his relationship, or whatever you wanted to call it, with Diana was anything like what Noah had with Lucia? His friend and sister had known each other for years and had been through a lot together. What did he have with Diana?

"Woman troubles, Rafe?"

He grunted. Noah had always been an intuitive bastard. It was part of what had made him such a great assassin.

"I'm just not sure I can trust her. She's different from any woman I've ever met. Nothing between us has unfolded in the usual way, and I'm not sure how to handle her."

Noah was quiet for a while. Rafe didn't rush him. From experience, he knew that Noah liked to look at things from all angles before he offered an opinion.

"Do you think she cares about you? Because in my experience, when the woman you care about lies, it's because she's scared. Your girl have a reason to be scared?"

"Yeah, but she doesn't trust me enough to tell me

why yet. Some asshole hurt her. Right now she's not telling me a thing about him."

"Until then, it might not be a bad idea to put a tracker on her."

As soon as Noah suggested it, Rafe wondered why he hadn't already done it. Damn, he was getting soft already. "Definitely doing that today."

"I can give you ideas for some really good trackers that she won't even notice. But most important, keep your eyes on her. You've always had crazy good instincts. If there's even a chance that this girl is into something bad, you might be her only chance to get out of it alive."

DIANA TOOK another bite of her pad thai and chewed mindlessly, not tasting a thing. She glanced over at Rafe. This had been the weirdest day. Ever since they'd woken up, she'd been getting a weird vibe from him. It wasn't that he'd treated her any differently or ignored her, but the previous open, raw intensity she'd gotten from him was gone. *Cautious*. That was the best way she could describe the way he seemed now.

Like you're any better.

Diana put down her fork with a sigh. It was entirely possible that Rafe was just reacting to her shifting emotions. How was she supposed to reconcile the man responsible for her father's death with the same man who seemed hell-bent on protecting and sheltering her?

"Is it good?"

She jerked her gaze up at the sound of his voice. They'd been eating their takeout on the couch, watching a movie, but she hadn't paid attention to any of it. Rafe didn't look like he much cared about it either. He'd been sneaking glances over at her the whole time but hadn't said anything to her directly until now.

"Diana? Are you okay?" Rafe's eyes narrowed slightly as he looked her over.

"Yup. I'm great." She winced at the cheesy response. "Just really hungry."

His eyes dropped to her almost-full plate of food. She'd been pushing the same pile of noodles around for the past half hour. He didn't call her out on the obvious lie though, just took the plate from her and placed it carefully on the coffee table in front of them. Then he knelt on the floor at her feet and took her hand, her fingers small in his larger ones.

"Rafe, what are you doing?"

He moved forward until he was between her legs. She sucked in a breath as his body insinuated itself right between her thighs, brushing against her everywhere. The desire that had been simmering in the background burst forth and raced through her, stealing her breath. Damn, the man could just breathe and turn her on.

Diana tried to look away, but he put a finger under her chin and held her still so she couldn't avoid his eyes. Even that was sexy, the way he just took control and handled her. She wouldn't have thought she'd like that, especially coming from a background of such domineering men. But Rafe had a way of doing things that made her feel safe and protected instead of trampled over and ignored. Everything he did seemed to be for her benefit and pleasure.

Especially in the bedroom.

She blushed. The man definitely enjoyed putting her pleasure first and seemed to consider it a challenge to make her lose control.

"I'm talking to you. I'm making sure you know that you can tell me anything. *Anything.* I'm not going to judge you."

Diana bit her lip. It was so stupid that she had this sudden urge to cry. But he was being so sweet and gentle with her. Was it so wrong that she wished it could be real? That she wished they were just normal people who'd met one day and could actually have a relationship? Instead, he was a dangerous former assassin, and she was a stupid girl who'd actually believed she could investigate her father's death on her own. Her investigation was a joke because she still had no idea who had actually ordered her father's death, and worse, all she'd accomplished so far was falling halfway in love with Rafe.

Not that she thought Rafe was a saint. It was obvious that he was exactly who her research had revealed him to be. Lethal. But he seemed to use his not-quite-legal talents to help protect those who needed it instead of hurting others. So why hadn't he done the same for her father? Everything inside was screaming for her to make sense of this mystery.

Rafe was still watching her closely, his eyes scanning her face like he could hear her twisted thoughts. "Are you in trouble, Diana?"

"No, I'm fine. Why would you think I'm in trouble?" she answered automatically.

He looked disappointed but didn't say anything else, just rubbed her arms until she felt like purring. Diana let out a little sigh and then cleared her throat to cover it. It was dangerous to let down her guard with him. With him rubbing her like that and looking at her with his dark, liquid eyes, she'd be lucky if he didn't have her spilling all her secrets in no time.

"I'm going to tell you what I think is going on. Okay? You don't have to say anything, you can just listen."

She nodded to let him know she'd heard him, but

her tongue felt like it was glued to the roof of her mouth. His fingers were still dancing over her arms, and she was melting bit by bit with every stroke.

"You are a beautiful woman. I can see that you don't truly understand how beautiful you are. Women like you often end up with men who don't appreciate you. Men who take advantage of your sweet nature."

Rafe's voice was a quiet rumble between them, the gentle power of it making her feel so safe. Diana had no idea where he was going with this but couldn't ignore her body's response to him telling her she was beautiful. Her pussy clenched hard and her nipples drew up so tight that if he looked down, he'd be able to tell. *Calm down*, she thought, annoyed at the instant physical response. Her overeager nipples reacted like he was talking directly to them. Another wash of heat ran through her as she remembered how Rafe had worshipped her breasts every time they made love. It was no wonder her body reacted so quickly just to the sound of his voice.

"But you don't have to worry about that with me. I would never hurt you. All I want to do is protect you. I *need* to protect you. Do you understand?"

Diana pulled him closer and held him against her. He softened and folded himself around her. It was a completely unique feeling to want to curl up in his arms and just stay there forever. Before this, she wouldn't have thought herself a particularly emotional or demonstrative woman, but with Rafe all her vulnerable parts were flayed open, and worse, she was okay with it.

"You can't save me from this," she murmured. It was so tempting to confide in him and just tell him the whole story. But no matter how wonderful he was being right now, she had a lifetime of experience with her father and brothers, men who acted one way and then changed when you displeased them. She simply couldn't take the chance.

"He's not going to get anywhere near you, sweetheart. I would never allow anyone to hurt you."

Surprised at the fierce certainty in his voice, Diana pulled back slightly. What was he talking about?

"Some men have trouble letting go after a relationship, but that's no excuse for raising your hand to a woman. I'll never understand those types of men. How can you harm someone who trusts you?" Rafe brushed her hair back from her forehead and pressed a gentle kiss there.

Diana stared at him in confusion before she figured out he was talking about her fabricated boyfriend. The one she was supposed to be running from.

She flushed, startled to see how quickly she'd lost the

thread of her own lies. It was so easy to get caught up in this fairytale, to forget who she was and why she was really here. But she could never allow herself that luxury because Rafe wouldn't feel this way about her if he knew who she really was. People always talked about unconditional love, but there was no such thing. All love was conditional, based on the person being who you thought they were. All Rafe's love would turn to hate if he found out she'd come here with the sole purpose of exposing him to the authorities.

"I'm terrified," she said truthfully. The enormity of the situation she'd gotten herself into swelled up until it seemed larger than life itself. She buried her head in the curve of Rafe's shoulder, hoping he wouldn't see her tears.

"I wasn't there before, but I'm here now. You don't need to be scared ever again. None of that ugliness can touch you now."

"There's nothing you can do," she whispered, burying her face against his neck. "You can't protect me from this. No one can."

"I can. You have no idea the lengths I will go to for you, baby."

His endearment just made it worse. She couldn't even speak because there was nothing to say. Nothing would make this situation right except for turning back time and changing the past. Even that wouldn't help because then they never would have met.

They were just two people who weren't meant to be, and to Diana, that was the most heartbreaking thing of all.

10

This must be what it was like to have Stockholm Syndrome.

Except he's not your captor. You are choosing to be here. He is your prisoner. He just doesn't know it yet.

This was so fucked. Ever since the epic orgasms, it was harder to look at him the same way. If she was honest with herself, it had been hard to look at him the same way since she'd seen him with his family.

Rafe killed her father. Her intel told her that was the truth. So how was he *that* man and *this* man.

And how are you this woman... the kind of woman who could be with the man who killed her father? She kept telling herself she was doing what had to be done. But she knew the truth.

There was a part of her that liked him. Liked being in his arms.

Yeah, the vagina part. *Yeah, good plan. Keep sleeping with him. Get even more deeply involved with him. Make it worse.*

But one thing he was good at was making her feel safe. She could almost pretend. Pretend that he wasn't an assassin. Pretend that she was normal. She felt safe, protected, invincible, powerful. And she knew that was because of him. Because he was a really good liar.

What is he going to do when he realizes you've been lying to him?

Diana shoved aside the thought. She knew what would happen. She just had to get out of here before then. The real question was how much time did she have? She needed the truth. She had spent years of her life on this. She wasn't walking away until she had it. Even if it put her life at risk.

He might be deadly, but so was she. She could pretend for just a little while longer. Pretend that she was just a girl and Rafe was just a guy. A guy that gave mind-blowing orgasms like it was his job. Right now she was going to stay put. Stay put and pretend.

"Earth to Diana." Rafe squeezed her hand.

They had walked around the corner to a café to get pastries. A perfectly normal couple-thing to do. Except he was checking egress routes and keeping her protected from every angle. He was also a pro at keeping off the cameras.

Of course, he would know where they all were. Once an assassin, always an assassin.

"Yeah, I'm fine. Just thinking, you know. This whole thing is unexpected."

He nodded before lifting their intertwined hands to kiss hers. "It's no pressure, okay? Don't worry about it. We're just taking a Sunday stroll."

Yep. And she was checking her exit routes too. Before she'd executed her plan, she'd hidden money and weapons all over this neighborhood in case things got sticky. Her nearest stash was underneath that mailbox on the corner. She was uncomfortable leaving guns around, so she'd hidden a Taser and about two grand.

"I know." She forced herself to smile.

It was like the two of them were having a whole subtext conversation.

Rafe: I'm suspicious of you, but you're sexy, so let's bone.

Her: I don't trust you and I want answers, but you're really good at boning, so let's bone until I get my answers, and then I'm taking you down.

Rafe: You're welcome to try. And If I find out what you're lying about, I'm going to kill you.

Her: Not if I see it coming. I'll be in the wind.

Totally healthy relationship.

She changed the topic. "Tell me about where you grew up. Who you were."

His hand stilled for a breath of a moment, but then he stroked her hand with his thumb. "It's not that exciting."

"Come on. I want to know. You're so self-contained. I'd love a little glimpse into young Rafe."

He silently brushed his thumb over her skin for a moment, but when he spoke, his voice was low. "Well, you already know about my parents. My life is divided into two sections—before and after."

She understood that. "Okay. What were you like before?"

He shrugged. "I guess I was sort of invisible in a sea of other kids just like me. I was a good student, good athlete. My parents were pretty strict. Dad didn't fuck around, ya know? And if I'm being honest, I didn't want to disappoint them." He was silent for a moment. "After, things were... different."

"Did you change?"

"Had to. I had to become more responsible. I know Nonna was there, but I felt like I had to take care of Lucia. I needed to be there for her. I couldn't be quite so selfish."

"You were just a kid though."

"I didn't see it that way. She was younger. I'd had more time with Mom and Dad. I felt like I needed to give her some of what they'd given me growing up."

"I guess that makes sense."

"On the flip side, that neighborhood, it forced me to toughen up too. There was way more trouble than I'd ever been exposed to out in the burbs of Connecticut. In Brooklyn if I put a toe out of line, someone bigger and badder would beat my ass."

"So you learned to be the biggest and baddest, I'm assuming?"

He squeezed her tight. "You better believe it. In that neighborhood, it was kind of prison rules. You had to establish that it might not be a good idea to mess with you. And you had to do it quick."

She couldn't even fathom growing up like that. "How long did it take you?"

He chuckled. "Two days. Some kid was giving Lucia shit. So I kicked his ass. In all fairness, I was fucked up over my parents' deaths. I just didn't know it at the time. I also didn't know that the kid had an older brother. One who'd come looking for me."

She lifted her head to meet his gaze. "What happened?"

"He wanted to even the score." He shrugged nonchalantly. "I had a lot of pent-up anger."

"You poor kid."

"Nonna had already raised one hellion in my dad. She took me to martial arts class. It helped calm some of that anger. But I learned quickly that I couldn't stand for what I saw as injustice. I also learned that the martial arts would come in handy for... other things."

She could just see him righting wrongs. "What, you were the Equalizer?"

His lips tipped into a wry smirk. "I fashioned myself a superhero. In reality, I was just angry. I did some other stupid shit too. Too much stupid shit. I'm lucky I didn't end up dead."

"But you probably did some good."

"I like to think so. Once I settled down and took a look at the direction of my life, things were easier. I could access part of who I used to be. I got interested in school and sports again. It was a rough two years. But no one messed with Lucia or me."

"How did Nonna take that?"

He grinned. "She was a tough old lady even then. She knew what I was up to. As long as I didn't bring cops to her door and she knew I was safe, she let me do as I wanted. Knew that I had a firm sense of right and wrong. Even though I rode that line a few times, occasionally tipping my ass over, I corrected it." He played with a lock of her hair. "What about you? What was little Diana like?"

She sighed and tore her gaze from his, squeezing his hand. "I grew up in central Pennsylvania but we spent a lot of time in Austria where my Dad grew up. Two older brothers. Mom died when I was eight. That left me with the guys."

He studied her intently. "You must have missed her a lot."

She nodded even as she tried to blink back tears. "I did. Once she was gone, I was so lonely. My brothers basically ignored me. Which was fine, I guess. They had a cruel streak to them when they played, and I preferred my dolls not to be decapitated."

"Did you have a lot of friends?"

"Not really. I kept to myself a lot. Even when I went to college. I didn't relate well to kids my age. I think I was too serious for most of them. Too much in my own head. Aloof, maybe. Doesn't help that I speak my mind."

"*You* speak your mind? No way." He grinned.

She turned and bit him gently. His sharp intake of breath was low, charged, and it made her insides warm. The look he gave her said he'd happily back her against one of these buildings and sink into her.

"Careful now, little Diana. You bite me, and I'll bite you back."

She giggled and nipped him again. "I dare you."

"I see what you're doing. Trying to tempt me so you don't have to talk. I'll give you what you're asking for later, when we get back to the apartment, but we'll talk first."

She narrowed her gaze but kept walking. "So I don't have many friends, I guess."

"And boyfriends?" His question was quiet, but she heard the hint of ice and possessiveness in his words.

"Like I said, I have a hard time connecting. It's like everyone spoke one language and I spoke another. I wasn't too close to my father or brothers, so I had no real male role models. I practically begged for attention from them. I guess I carried those habits into my dating life and made some crap choices. It's like I've been searching for something, you know? Although it's not like I had a lot of boyfriends. One in college and one after."

He ran his hands over her hair. "You don't have to make those wrong choices anymore." He paused and tugged her to the edge of the sidewalk, then kissed her deep, and Diana's synapses fried.

His kisses dragged her into a lust-filled fog of denial and need. A place where she didn't have to think about the girl she once was. A place where she wasn't the lonely girl who just wanted someone to love.

The lonely girl whose father had been taken.

He cupped her cheek, gently stroking her skin as he kissed her. Diana knew she would never be the same after this. He was changing her. And she wasn't sure if it was for the best.

BACK IN THE apartment with their coffee and their pastries, Rafe tried to discern what she was thinking. Noah had to be right. She was evasive. Not exactly lying, but not eager to talk about her life. Maybe she was scared.

She needed to trust him. Had to know he'd help her with anything. He set the coffees down and tugged her close. "Listen, I know you're gun-shy. But no matter what, I won't let anything happen to you." He slowly slid his arms around her waist and pulled her into his body.

She nodded. "Y-yes. I know you wouldn't."

"Good." With a groan, he took her mouth under his, teasing with his tongue. And she opened for him on a sigh. She tasted like coffee and spice, and he never wanted to stop. He was spinning out. He needed her. Even as his brain told him to be careful, to go slow, his body and his heart dived in headfirst. She was his. He always protected what was his. He just had to convince her that she wanted to stay.

Rafe angled his head and deepened the kiss, dipping his tongue into her mouth, drawing hers out playfully. As he teased her, she looped her arms around his neck and brought her body into close contact with his, rubbing her nipples against his chest.

He snuck his hand under her T-shirt, and she rocked her hips against him. With his thumb, he teased a circular pattern around her belly button.

She was so soft everywhere, with skin like satin. He could spend hours touching her, savoring every inch of her skin, but her breathy moans urged him on. Sliding his hands up her torso, he let his thumbs graze the underside of her breasts, and the rest of the blood in his brain migrated south. His cock throbbed painfully against his thigh, and he bit back a curse.

He traced his thumbs over the lace of her bra to the taut nipples beneath. With a frustrated snarl, he picked her up and settled her on the counter. She started to quiver when he stroked his thumbs over her nipples. When he closed his palm over her full breast, Diana slid her hands into his hair and tugged. Her nails scoring over his scalp sent a shiver through him.

Diana rocked her body against his, and the thick, pulsing lust coursing in his veins made it impossible to think. He craved more. *Needed* more. His hips jerked—

he was so desperate to get closer, to be inside her and possess her.

"Wrap your legs around me, Diana," he muttered before sucking on her bottom lip. When she didn't, he teased her lip with his teeth. "Did you hear me, sweetheart?"

"Yeah, I just can't seem to move."

With a chuckle, he helped her into position, then moved them over to the couch. He levered over her, then slowly eased his weight down on top of her, his throbbing dick directly against her core.

Rafe lifted the hem of her shirt. Her smooth skin beckoned. Trailing kisses down her neck, he sought out one of her nipples. Through the lace fabric of her bra, he suckled and drew her in deep with his tongue and lips, then with the barest hint of teeth, he grazed the peak. Diana bucked beneath him, and his cock begged for relief.

He teased first one nipple, licking it, suckling it, while his fingers played with the tip of the other. Every tug sent a stab of lust through his body.

But he couldn't get enough of her. Finally he pulled her into a semiseated position and tugged her shirt over her head. The bra followed in short order, and Rafe forgot to breathe. Her breasts, full and heavy with dusky rose tips, beckoned to him. He laid her back gently and settled himself directly between her thighs again.

Diana raised her hips, rubbing against him like a cat. Each time her heated center came in contact with the rigid length of him, he struggled for control, but he didn't know how much longer he could hold on.

Ragged breaths tore from his chest. "Diana, please stop moving. I really want to be inside you when I come."

Beneath him, she whimpered. "So close though."

He bit back a groan as she wiggled again. "You don't listen too well." Rafe dipped his head, breathing over the perfect peak of her breast. With every movement over her nipple with the stubble of his chin, her hips lifted and she reached for him. She gasped when he secured one nipple and sucked her deep into his mouth.

Diana threw her head back and moaned his name when he suckled harder. Desire thickened his blood as she held him to her. He ached with the need to be inside her.

His hand at her hip, he traced the line of her thong under the cotton of her leggings. He tugged gently, and as fabric gave way to silky skin, he kissed the path of sinful heaven exposed to him. First her hip, then the divot where her leg met joint. Then her belly button.

Diana lifted her hips to aid him as he removed her

leggings. He discarded them somewhere over his head and then swiftly yanked his shirt off. With trembling fingers, she reached up and traced the pads of her fingertips over his abdomen.

"You realize you look airbrushed, right?"

Rafe choked out a strangled laugh as he nuzzled her belly button again. "What?"

She nodded. "Someone overdid it with the photoshopping of your muscles."

"I promise you, they're all real." He kissed his way back up her body. When he reached her lips, he took his time savoring her. Everything about her taste careened him toward orgasm. The way her tongue met his, even as he dipped and retreated into her mouth, simulating how else he wanted to join their bodies, how he wanted to stroke into her with his cock.

His fingers stole under the fabric of her panties, and excitement ripped at him. He knew what came next. Her dewy slickness. Her sex tugging at him while he explored.

As he slid a finger inside her heat, they both gasped, and the base of his spine tingled. *Shit.* He wasn't even inside her, and he was so ready to blow.

He wanted to tease an orgasm out of her, and he wanted to take his time doing it. But it seemed like Diana had other plans. Working her hand between them, she pulled on his belt. Once she yanked it through the loops and tossed it away, she unbuttoned his jeans. Rafe watched intently as her graceful hand slowly tugged his zipper down.

When Diana slid her hand into his jeans, he stopped breathing. *Oh hell.* Delicate fingers wound around his erection, and all higher functioning stopped. All his focus went to where her sweet core milked his finger and her fingers milked him.

She stroked him again, and his brain shut down. All he registered was the warm silk of her palm caressing the straining head of his dick. She lingered over the head, using her thumb to spread the moisture gathered there and teasing the hypersensitive ridge.

Rafe squeezed his eyes shut. The urge to come was a strong, beating pulse in his malfunctioning brain. *Come. She wants you to come. You know you want to.* Each beat of his heart sent thick, lust-laced blood through his veins straight to his dick.

She watched his response from under a hooded gaze. When she licked her lips, he gave serious thought to begging her to wrap her lips around him so he could get some relief. But he was torn. He also wanted to prolong the feeling, prolong that sex-crazed current running through his body and making him hum.

The firm pressure she applied on each downstroke

of his length sent fiery tingles down his spine, and he stilled her hand.

He dropped his forehead to hers. "Jesus, I want to come so bad."

She slowed her pace but didn't stop. Leaning in, she whispered, ""Isn't that the point?"

She was going to kill him. "Diana... inside you... fuck." Ragged breaths tore from his chest. "This way—" No matter how many ways he tried to rev the engine, his brain refused to come online. "I... I..." But then her inner walls clamped tight around his fingers and there was a slight quiver. It reminded him that he wanted to see her come more than he wanted to come himself.

Snapping his free hand around her wrist, Rafe shook his head. "Oh, no you don't. Ladies first. *Always*. You keep touching me or, God help me, make that face like you're wondering how I taste, and I'll forget that."

"You're the only one who gets to explore?" She pouted.

He stroked a thumb over her clit, and Diana threw her head back. "Oh, you'll get your turn, I promise."

"Rafe..." Her voice was thready.

God, she was so sexy. "Open your legs wider."

Diana complied without question and dug her nails into the flesh on his shoulders. "Rafe, please..."

With another flutter of his thumb, she broke apart,

her mouth open on a silent scream. He watched her in awe, a smug grin spreading over his face. That was what he'd been waiting for.

He kissed her again, licking into her mouth, and he stoked the flame in her body to full roar. He slid his tongue over and against hers, tasted every corner of her, and coaxed her tongue into a game of chase.

He slid his hands down over her backside and picked her up. Walking them down the hall to his bedroom and over to the bed, he didn't break the kiss. With every adjustment of positioning, he angled his head and delved back in for another kiss, desperate to devour her.

He bent over, and when her back hit the mattress and he lowered some of his weight onto her, it brought his now-throbbing cock directly into contact with the part of her that ached for him. Diana groaned.

As they kissed, he ran his hands over her face and dug them into her thick hair, occasionally tugging a little, letting her know he wasn't always under control.

He reached over to the nightstand, unwilling to break the kiss. When he found a condom, he impatiently tore it open. On a muttered curse, he tore his lips away from hers so he could kick off his jeans properly and sheathe himself. But his lips were back on hers in seconds.

As he kissed her, he rocked his body into hers, the bite of electricity slamming into him as he sank into her. She lifted her hips to meet his and Rafe was lost. Instinct took over as he made love to her. In his head a distant voice reminded him of what he'd known all along. *Mine.*

When he felt the telltale flutter and quiver over his cock, he drew back so he could watch her face. Her gaze met his as the orgasm rolled into her, and in that one look, Rafe knew he wasn't going to be able to say goodbye.

All he could do was hold on twice as hard as he finally let go and his release rocketed him into oblivion.

11

The next day Rafe drove to Blake Security for the workout he'd been neglecting. Despite his decision to retire from the FBI, his body was his weapon, and he couldn't afford to allow his blade to go dull.

Especially now that you have someone to protect.

He felt a sense of bone-deep *right* at the thought. No matter what happened, no matter what he discovered about what Diana was hiding, she'd triggered his protective instincts something crazy. He had to keep her safe. For the first time since his rebirth—the way he thought of getting out of the FBI and reclaiming his rightful identity—he had something that was just his.

Nonna and Lucia had formed a strong family bond while he was gone, and rightfully so. They'd gone on with their lives, and he wouldn't have wanted anything less for them. But that didn't mean it wasn't painful to observe how close they were and how many private jokes and experiences existed between them that he simply wasn't a part of. They didn't need him anymore.

His cheeks warmed as he thought about everything he'd told her yesterday. His childhood wasn't something he ever discussed. It was easier not to be bitter over what he'd lost if he didn't revisit it. But when he was with Diana, he felt like she was used to being on the outskirts just like he was.

And it made him feel like his luck was finally changing.

Then he looked up and saw Alan watching him from across the room. Rafe bit back a curse. His good luck wouldn't hold, it would seem.

He grabbed his phone and dialed Matthias. "Did you guys lose something?"

Matthias sighed. "Not my fault, mate. I tried to warn you. You didn't answer. Noah told him to go on back." Then he hung up.

Rafe growled even though he knew it wasn't the kid's fault. Noah knew that Alan had been his handler for years, but he didn't know that Rafe was trying to avoid him.

Once he realized Rafe had seen him, Alan walked across the gym mats, dodging around the exercise balls and the scattered treadmills and other equipment. With a team of security professionals, many of whom lived on site, Noah had made sure to have a professionally equipped gym.

"Rafe. You look well. I thought you were going to take some time off? You know, go on a vacation. Wear flowered shirts and gain a few pounds." Alan chuckled at his own joke.

Rafe picked up a heavier weight and started curling. "I'm not letting myself go, if that's what you're asking. What do you want, Alan?"

The other man's sigh said it all. "We really need your help on this Vandergraff case. You have insight that we just can't get from paperwork. The more you dodge this, the more questions Interpol has. I think if you just made yourself available for questions—"

"I told you I'd search for information, but beyond that, I'm not getting involved. That part of my life is over." Rafe let the weight in his hand fall to the floor of the gym where it landed with a dull thud.

Suddenly he was irrationally angry. He'd done everything the FBI had asked of him. Sacrificed his life, his name, his relationships with his family, and essentially every dream he'd had as a young man about what his future would look like. There was no expectation of a thank-you.

Uncle Sam, like any other organization, didn't spare much appreciation for the workers at the bottom that made the gears turn. But Rafe didn't feel it was too much to expect some peace in his retirement from the bureau. He'd served honorably, and now he was ready to move on.

But how could he move on when he still felt the weight of his old life around his neck?

Alan blew out a breath. ""You might not have a choice here. This doesn't look good, Rafe."

"What doesn't look good?"

"You know how things are at the bureau. If the wrong people start asking questions, a small thing can turn into an international incident. With you being so cagey about this, people are starting to ask questions about why a former agent is living life so large after retiring so young."

Now that pissed him off. "Living large? How am I living large? I'm not flashy. I don't spend a lot of money. I know how to keep a low profile."

Suddenly Alan didn't look so sure of himself anymore. "You make a lot of money for a security consultant. You've got a nice place that you own outright and several expensive vehicles. It looks bad, man, especially since you aren't even working regular shifts here."

Alan glanced around. "Whatever the hell a regular shift around here looks like."

"You have me under surveillance or something?"

Alan didn't meet his eyes. "Look, this case is too big to ignore. Solving it would make anyone's career. People are not going to stop digging."

Rafe smiled. "You think I stole it, don't you?"

He shook his head sadly. After all the years he'd put in, they still didn't trust him. They always said there was no honor among thieves. It seemed there was no honor among the enforcers of the law either. Not that he'd ever drunk that particular Kool-Aid. The guys on the so-called "right" side of the law were often cut from the same cloth as the guys they were chasing.

"I didn't take that diamond, Alan. You guys are wasting your time."

"I know that," Alan assured him hastily. "But they don't know you like I do. I'm trying to help you, Rafe. But you have to help me too."

"That's where you're wrong," Rafe replied before turning to nail Alan with a direct look. "I don't have to do shit. Now leave. And don't show up at my place of business again."

Alan shook his head. "You're making a mistake."

"Maybe. It wouldn't be the first time."

Rafe watched him go and then cursed as soon as

he'd left the room. Alan might be gone, but that didn't mean this was the end of it.

He needed to do some digging of his own.

WHAT THE HELL was happening to her life?

Diana finished wiping the counter in the kitchen and then sat down at the dining table.

It was a little pathetic, but she'd gotten so used to spending her days and nights with Rafe that it was kind of weird now that he wasn't here. She should be jumping for joy. He'd left her alone in the apartment so he could go to the gym. This was what she'd been waiting for, a sign of trust.

An opportunity.

But despite the fact that she'd gotten what she'd been hoping for, Diana felt curiously empty.

That's because you're acting like a silly little girl with a crush instead of an intelligent, calculating woman with a plan.

Warmth spread through her at the thought of the prior night in Rafe's arms. Shame and desire battled, but she couldn't deny that things had changed between them. There was something about the way he looked at her, touched her, and held her. She'd never experienced anything like this before, and she couldn't believe that something this right could happen if he really was a coldhearted killer.

Diana pressed her hands to her cheeks. She was supposed to be avenging her father's death, and instead all she was doing was questioning everything she thought she knew. Rafe was the killer, there was no way she could have gotten that wrong. Being so young when her father was killed, there was always the risk that time had warped her memory of the event, but there was no mistaking those eyes. It had been Rafe in the office with her father. She'd never forget the sight of those eyes from behind his mask. Not to mention that she'd seen him in action since coming here.

Her mind wasn't playing tricks on her. Rafe DeMarco was lethal and absolutely capable of murder. But the man she'd come to know since arriving here operated under strict codes of honor. He was principled.

Which made no sense!

Diana groaned. The only way she could make things add up was to find the clues she was looking for and figure out the real story. Maybe there had been a reason that Rafe had been there. Could her father have been set up? Maybe someone else had framed him for something. Rafe didn't hurt people indiscriminately, so he must have been led to believe her father was guilty of something.

You're just trying to rationalize it.

The thought that she was going soft when she should be avenging the only man who'd ever loved her brought on a wave of despair. Diana stood reluctantly and made her way into the living room. She started with the windows, inspecting all the sills before moving to the artwork again. Now that she knew he had motion sensors on the paintings, she didn't dare take any of them down.

With a frustrated little sigh, she swept her eyes over the rest of the apartment. He didn't spend a lot of time in the kitchen, and she'd already searched that room thoroughly anyway under the guise of "cooking." The only places she hadn't had time to search were his bedroom and the office.

Starting with the bedroom, she swept her hands under the mattress and peered under the bed frame. The ceilings and walls were smooth, with no indication that any areas had been punched out and patched, so she doubted he'd hidden anything in the walls. How would she retrieve it anyway?

Oh, don't mind the mess, Rafe. I just wanted to check out the other side of your drywall!

Diana shook her head at the thought. Now that she

was gaining his trust, she didn't want to do anything overt that would cause her to lose it. He would eventually give away a clue; it was inevitable. She just had to be patient.

Giving up on the bedroom, she walked down the hall to the office. She'd never been in that room before, only seen inside when he'd left the door open. It was decorated in typical male fashion with dark paint on the walls and lots of leather. She sat in the desk chair, inhaling the scent of Rafe.

Focus.

She traced under the surface of the desk, feeling for any grooves or cracks where something could be hidden. Nothing. She shook the mouse, but when the computer screen flared to life, it showed only the passcode screen. Well, it was worth a try. She could always hope that maybe he was an assassin with lax security standards at home.

There was another painting in here too. She didn't recognize the artist this time. She quickly checked the shelves and the walls, then lastly looked for any levers or buttons in the frame of the painting. Nothing.

Sighing, she left the office and went back to her room.

She was just about to walk back out into the hallway when she heard Rafe's voice. He must have come home. She had been listening for him, but the man moved like a cat. Maybe she should tie a bell around his dick. That way she'd know every time he was around.

Who was he talking to? Rafe didn't seem to have many friends outside of his work and family.

Taking a chance, she crept closer to the door just in time to see Rafe appear at the entrance to the hallway.

He glanced around, eyes narrowed. Then took a step back to look in the kitchen.

He was looking for her, she realized.

She ducked back into her room and heard his murmurs as he walked by her room. He was making sure she didn't overhear him. Which meant he was discussing something he didn't want her to know about.

This was her chance. Now or never. It was either follow him or be stuck in this limbo.

She tiptoed after him.

RAFE'S PHONE started ringing while he was on the way home.

"What's up, Noah?" He figured the other man had probably heard about his annoyance from Matthias by now.

"I meant to grab you before you left. We need your help investigating a potential new hire."

That was news. Rafe had no question about his place in the company. He was like a precision blade, used when needed. But he hadn't been invited to participate in many other ways. Despite how things seemed, he was still getting back on even ground with Noah. They were still moving around each other, trying to figure out where the pieces fit in their new relationship. It was odd for Rafe to be so uncertain around the man he'd taken under his wing a decade ago and trained from the ground up. But in the time he'd been gone, Noah had matured into the kind of strong leader Rafe had always known he would be.

Which was why being asked for help meant more to him than Noah would ever know.

"Not sure what I can do, but whatever you need, you know I'm there," he finally answered, hoping his rough voice didn't betray the depth of feeling.

"This guy is former ORUS. Call sign *Lynx*. Did you know him?"

Rafe's brow furrowed as he thought back. He'd definitely never worked directly with the guy. Before taking any tandem assignment, he'd always memorized the file on the other agent, looking for vulnerabilities or weaknesses. He'd definitely remember if they'd worked together.

"I never worked with him. Although, that doesn't mean I don't have anything on him."

Noah laughed. "Of course. Your file of secrets. I'd almost forgotten that you kept information on everyone. You always were a paranoid bastard."

"It's served me well. Let me take a look at what I have in my files. If he's mentioned, even in a peripheral way, I'll let you know."

Rafe pulled into the garage for his building and parked. He cradled his phone between his neck and his ear while grabbing the gym bag on the passenger seat.

"While you're doing that, I wanted to ask about earlier. Matthias mentioned that you seemed less than happy to see Alan."

Here we go, Rafe thought. He should have known he hadn't escaped Noah's attention.

The guy had been a top ORUS operative for a reason.

"Yeah. The FBI has a different definition of retired than I do, apparently." Rafe opened the door to his apartment and dropped his bag by the door.

"Are they pressuring you to come back?"

"Nothing I can't handle."

Noah was quiet for a moment. "You've given them

enough of your life. Lucia would be devastated if you left again."

Rafe paused midstep. "I would never do that to her. I promise. My days of disappearing are over."

Suddenly realizing just how loud he was talking, Rafe paused, glancing into the kitchen and then behind him into the living room. Diana liked to burrow into the cushions of the couch while watching TV and sometimes fell asleep there. He shouldn't be talking about disappearing so cavalierly when she could overhear. His shoulders dropped in relief when he didn't see her. She was probably taking a shower. He walked down the hall to his office.

"Good. You're an important part of this family. Izzy is going to need her uncle around to help keep her safe. Especially if she grows up anything like her mother and her aunt JJ."

Rafe snorted and pushed open the door to his office. Immediately, all his senses went on alert.

Someone had been in here.

"Hold on, Noah. I need to check my files." He put the phone on mute.

Rafe glanced around, noting that nothing was out of place. He shook off the weird feeling. None of his alarms had been triggered, and he'd know if someone had entered or left the apartment. He just wasn't used to having another person in his house. It would take some getting used to, having a feminine scent lingering all around.

He pressed against the painting that hid his safe. After entering the code, he started pulling out the files. He had information saved on a thumb drive, but there were certain things he also kept in printed copies. He knew how digital data could be corrupted. After glancing through quickly, he didn't see anything relevant. Closing the safe, he stood and took the phone off mute.

"Nothing. I've got nothing on him, but that doesn't mean he's clean. I can do some digging if you want."

"Let's do that. If we're going to bring someone new on board, I need to make sure they're safe to have around the girls."

Rafe instantly moved the task to the top of his priority list. Anyone who would have that much access to his sister and his niece would have to pass muster with him first.

Rafe walked down the hallway, wondering in earnest where Diana was. She'd been cleaning up after breakfast when he'd left.

It was kind of pathetic, actually, that he missed her. He'd only been gone two hours. He shook his head.

"I hear you. You know I don't want anyone who isn't trustworthy near Lucia and Izzy either."

Noah chuckled. "Why do you think I called you? You're the only one in the universe who might be as overprotective of them as I am." He paused. "You know if the FBI is giving you trouble, you can tell me, right?"

Rafe clutched the phone tighter. "It's all good. You don't need to make any enemies on my behalf."

Noah paused. "I will if necessary."

12

Diana had already mapped the hallway. She knew exactly where the floor creaked. She knew exactly what would make a sound. First rule when you were following a known killer down the hallway while he was having a conversation he obviously did not want you to hear—discretion.

On tiptoes, she crept toward his office door.

But what doesn't he want you to hear? Honestly, it could be anything. It could be his doctor. It could be some ex. Oh shit. Did he have children?

Hello, focus.

She leaned closer and realized it was someone from Blake Security on the phone. They wanted him to check files on someone. Why was he the one checking files?

Wasn't that what Matthias was for? She'd never seen a hacker with such defined muscles before in her life.

The guy was smoking hot. *Yes, but why does he have the same tattoos as Noah and Rafe? Why did no one else at the party have them?*

Never mind all that. His sole purpose was to look things up, right? They'd all been teasing him at the party. If he could find anything on anyone, why was he calling Rafe?

"Yeah, I'd say take him on, but on a probationary period. No access to anything. Biometrics in the house, obviously. We'll only give him access in certain areas and limit his exposure to the baby until we dig deeper and he's seen the shrink. I mean, the guy is ex-ORUS, and given our recent experience, he's an unknown quantity."

ORUS? What the hell was ORUS? But she was too distracted by what Rafe was doing to dig down that rabbit hole. Through the crack in the door, she watched as he walked to the far wall and then gently pressed part of the painting.

Holy shit.

She'd been trying to see behind the damn thing. There'd been no buttons on the sides or hidden in the frame. She hadn't thought to actually physically touch the painting. When the painting slid up, it revealed a complicated-looking safe. It looked like the kind of thing that drug dealers in movies kept their cash in.

So if I were an assassin, what would I keep hidden away?

The possibilities were endless. Endlessly terrifying. Her mind helpfully conjured up images of monsters from movies and fiction. Everyone from Dexter to Corleone to Escobar. For all she knew, he was some insane version of all three. There could be a horse's head and cocaine in there.

Which is why you need to be sure.

Clearly, with that kind of security measure, he didn't want anyone accessing whatever it was. And that was precisely *why* she needed access to whatever the hell was in there. She was no safe expert, but when she was preparing for this little walk on the get-her-ass-killed side, she'd asked Charisse to contact her brother, who was some kind of computer expert. He'd reached out to some contract technical geniuses. For a hefty price, they'd found her an encryption device that could crack most security panels and safe keys. All that was needed was time—*lots* and lots of time. But maybe she'd get lucky. At least she knew where the safe was now. All she had to do was go get the decoder from Charisse's.

As Rafe wrapped up his conversation, she tiptoed back down the hall. Then once she hit the living room, she catapulted herself over the couch. The man was huge, but he moved quick. She didn't want to be up and about, giving him a reason to be suspicious.

You mean like he already is? Those little innocuous questions, the gentle probing—he knew something was up. Or suspected she wasn't being truthful. Either way, she needed to watch her step or she was going to end up like her father.

Good thing she had moved quickly too, because less than a minute later, Rafe was back in the living room.

His voice was a low, amused rumble. "There you are. Looking for something to watch?"

"No, not really. All that's on are crappy reality shows. And let me tell you, the Kardashians aren't so interesting that I need to keep up with them in reruns too. I have my credit cards, so it's probably time to head to the bookstore. I'll need a permanent address to get a library card."

He frowned. "I'll give you whatever you need."

"Rafe, you've already been generous enough. You've given me *everything*. I'm not one of those women who needs someone to take care of her. At least not before—" She deliberately cut herself off and didn't reveal too much. "I can stand on my own two feet."

"No one's saying you can't. I'm just saying if you want to get some books, we can make that happen."

"Thank you. I—" She sighed and wrapped her arms

around her knees, tucking them under her chin. "I'm really grateful. I'm fumbling the gratitude, I know. I just wanted to say thank you for everything. I don't know where I would be if you hadn't come along. Things probably would have turned out much, much worse."

Diana watched him warily. Did he suspect? Did he believe her? The man was like the sphinx, so goddamn difficult to read. *Well, that's what happens when you get in the den with killers.* They were really good at lying. And they made excellent hunters. Right now, she didn't know if she was the hunter or the hunted.

He cocked his head. "Is everything okay?"

She nodded. "It is. Thanks to you, I now have everything I need." And she did. As soon as he was at Blake Security, she was getting into that safe. Thanks to letting her vajayjay do the thinking, she'd lost sight of who she was and what she'd come to do.

She'd been distracted by his tongue and his fingers, and well, all that. Getting that close to him had been a mistake. But she was going to remedy that.

She knew where the safe was now. And it was just the reminder that she needed that Rafe DeMarco was a killer, not someone she could make into her boyfriend. "Everything is exactly as it should be."

RAFE WATCHED Diana as she pushed her hips back and up into downward dog.

Damn. Way to get a rise out of him. He'd just showered after his conversation with Noah, but he was so down for another shower. "You know, you could have worked out with me."

She laughed. "Uh, how do you think that would have turned out?" she asked him as she pushed her hips back again.

Oh fuck. His cock pressed against the fly of his jeans as if hearing his call to arms. "Well, I have one or two ideas."

"I'm sure you do. I actually wanted to get some yoga in. If I'd gone with you, you would have had your hands on my ass, and neither of us would have gotten a workout."

He grinned. "Oh, we'd have gotten a workout all right. And you would have been just as relaxed as with yoga."

She snorted and fluidly switched into triangle pose. "I'm trying to concentrate here. You're distracting me."

He chuckled. "Not yet, but that can be arranged. How do you feel about naked yoga?"

She slid him some serious side-eye. She was clearly teasing, but there was some tension to her posture. Something was off. She'd been fine before he left for the gym. Was she really fine? Had that asshole contacted her?

He'd been tracking her. She'd gone out to a couple of shops but had stayed in the neighborhood or at the apartment. She hadn't been far. Maybe she was scared like Noah had suggested.

Rafe's anger bubbled just under the surface. What had that piece of shit done to her that she was too scared to venture out? When he got his hands on that asshole, he was going to kill him.

Careful. You don't do that anymore, remember? Well for some cases, Libra could be resurrected.

When she shifted into a position on the floor, facing him with her legs up and open in a *V*, he groaned. "Seriously, are you trying to kill me?"

Her lips tipped up in a smirk. "Do you feel like you're dying? How do I intensify that feeling? Do you think I could kill you with sex?"

Cock… steel. Her voice dripped with pure sex and… a hint of danger. Like she might be a little serious. And shit, that just turned him on more. There was something so seriously wrong with him that he got off on the fact that she might try to kill him.

Sleep with the devil and you become a demon yourself.

Rafe stalked over to her and bent to kiss her. There

was a challenge in her eyes, but as soon as his lips touched hers, she went pliant and soft.

"I'd die happy," he mumbled against her lips.

He could feel it then, the tension easing out of her body. She gave him a soft moan and he eased her back, covering her body with his. God, she was so sexy.

She was hesitant at first, but then she looped her arms around his neck and splayed her thighs to make room for him. Rafe slid a hand into her hair and gave her a gentle tug to angle her the way he wanted.

He could feel it the moment desire tripped over her skin. She arched into him and moaned as he rocked his hips into her. "Fuck, that's it. Give it to me. Stop fighting it."

Suddenly she'd gone from cool to desperate as she met the shallow rocks of his hips. Her hands threaded through his hair and she held his head to her as if she'd given herself permission to want him.

Diana met each lick of his tongue with one of her own. She followed his lead but gave as good as she got. She wanted this. She tasted like honey and vanilla. She tasted like home.

Soon they were going to talk about next steps. Because he'd be damned if he was going to keep wondering if she'd be there when he came home. He'd gotten so used to having her around, letting go was going to be a bitch. *And maybe you don't have to.* He was going to fight to make that a reality. He just had to get her used to the idea.

Diana moaned, her hands roaming over his shoulders. His blood simmered just under his skin. *Hell yes.* This was what he needed. *Find out the truth before it's too late.* He shoved away that thought. For once he wasn't going to overthink everything.

She slid her hand between them and palmed his dick. It felt so good he saw stars. "Fuck, Diana—"

Naked, you have to get her naked. Right the fuck now.

His thumb rolled over her nipple and gently plucked the tight bud.

"Oh God, Rafe. Right there, just, please."

There was a distant ding that barely registered in his consciousness. Diana was in his blood, under his skin. Clawing her way into his soul. There was another ding and then a sharp rapping at his door.

Fuck. Who the hell was at his door?

The part of him that had been trained to kill, trained to survive, twitched, wanting to reach for his gun, his knives, and a rocket launcher.

But shit, Diana was pumping his dick, and Rafe DeMarco, the man, was so fucking desperate to slide home deep. Funny thing about desire—it made you stupid.

Every man on the planet would almost always choose to fuck over his own survival.

He was almost glad ORUS had trained that out of him when the series of dings on the phone alerted him.

He dragged his lips off hers and cursed under his breath. "Fuck. I need to get that."

"What?" Her voice was soft, breathy, and desperate. "You're going to leave me like this?"

Dick: The hell I am.

Assassin Brain: Two bullets through the door while you're fucking her takes care of both problems.

Rational Rafe: "I'm sorry baby, I need to get that. Hold that thought."

"That's not what I was holding."

With a frustrated growl, he jogged to the door. He didn't need to check his phone. He knew who it was. The last person he'd ever expected to find on his doorstep.

Rafe yanked the door open. "Matthias, what the fuck do you want?"

The kid smirked. "I was in the neighborhood. And I have the information you want. You left in such a hurry I didn't get to give it to you. Noah said I'm supposed to play nice. This is me playing nice." His gaze slid past Rafe to Diana inside and he grinned. "Did I interrupt?"

Assassin Rafe: Get out the knives and let's play.

Rational Rafe: Punch him in the face and go fuck.

Rafe sighed. "You could have mentioned you were coming around."

The kid shrugged. "I could have, but this way I get a chance to say hi to Diana." He brushed past Rafe and whistled. "Nice flat, mate. Gosh, I have interrupted something. It wasn't something important, was it?"

"Fuck you," Rafe growled.

Matthias chuckled. "Sorry. Not sorry." He sauntered over to a now-standing Diana and gave her a hug that lasted too long in Rafe's opinion. "Diana, love. You all right?" Rafe knew the kid had proximity issues. He was a cagey fuck who didn't like to be touched too often, but still, he was standing in Rafe's living room with his arms around Rafe's woman.

Relax. He's trying to get a rise out of you. Rafe could only scowl.

Diana grinned up at Matthias. "I'm good. It's good to see you."

"You know, Rafe's never invited any of us over before. We just show up uninvited. It's nice to actually receive a warm welcome for once." Matthias smirked at Rafe. "And the place looks better than ever. I don't doubt that you had something to do with it. I can't really see him buying pillows."

"I thought I'd help make the place cheery since he's been so nice to let me stay for a bit."

That was enough. Rafe nodded at Matthias. "You need to tell me something?"

Matthias chuckled. "Yeah, let's talk."

Rafe inclined his head. "This way." The kid was still angry at him. Good God, the Blake guys were such pussies. They all needed to get over the trying-to-kill-them thing.

That *one* time.

Okay, maybe twice. But so what? They were all friends now. Jonas and Oskar had warmed to him. But it seemed Matthias still held a grudge. Maybe because he'd bested the kid in hand-to-hand?

Rafe would never admit it to anyone, but he still felt a twinge of guilt when he thought back to the lengths he'd gone to rescue his sister... who hadn't needed rescuing at all. He'd let out that part of himself he swore was gone for good.

Rafe led Matthias into the office and closed the door behind them. "Okay, what's up?"

Rafe had never seen the kid smile this much. He looked positively giddy to have fucked up his night. "Okay. I did as you asked. I looked up Diana. It's like she said. She's from Yonkers, no points on her driver's license, and no debt to speak of. Granted, there's not really anything before three years ago when she graduated university. But she was a minor before that. So if there was anything, that's a little harder to find. I can do it if you want. But I'll only be able to find stuff specifically on her if she was registered in public school or had a run-in with law enforcement. Anything else I find will be on her parents and any family she has to speak of. You want me to dig deeper?"

Rafe frowned. She'd been telling the truth? Despite what Matthias was saying, everything in Rafe told him there was more to the story. "Yeah. Keep looking." The words came out clipped.

"You look tense, mate."

"Fuck you."

"If you're into that, I won't judge. Maybe Diana would like—"

Rafe was across the room in seconds, ready to level the kid, but he stopped short. In a split second, the shutters had fallen over Matthias's eyes, making them go dead. In an instant he'd gone from the teasing swagger of a friend to the cold façade of a killer. If Rafe touched him, there would be blood. A lot of it.

While Rafe didn't make a move, he kept direct eye contact and held his ground, showing him that he wasn't fazed but also wasn't aggressive. After several breaths, the kid seemed to shake off the killer and then averted his gaze.

Shit. Whatever had happened to the guy, that killer was never far away. He was there, always ready. Poised, waiting. The kid could be dangerous. But Rafe also saw the horror and remorse in those eyes as Matthias had wrestled the killer back into his chains. Hell, what had he survived?

Matthias's voice was quiet as he said, "As to the boyfriend, I found him. Let me tell you, that wasn't easy without a name, but they shared a lease together. He works at McLean Law Associates. He's pretty much a low-level messenger. Basic courier stuff. So if he ever did find her, the job allows enough leeway for him to come after her."

"Address?" Rafe asked through clenched teeth.

Matthias rattled it off. "I texted it to you already. You want us to handle it? This is sort of what we do, and usually no one ends up dead."

Read: You kill too much. Yeah, but so do you, kid.

"Thanks, but I'll be dealing with this myself."

Read: Sometimes people need to get dead. And I'm afraid to unleash your monster.

Matthias nodded. "I'll go."

Before the kid opened the door, Rafe called out.

"Kid, listen. I—" Fuck, what could he say? "If you need to talk to someone who gets it, I'm around."

Matthias's gaze met his, and Rafe saw the understanding there. "Yeah, I hear you."

That exchange was the best either of them had to offer.

When Matthias was gone, Diana stalked up to Rafe. "So, where were we?"

"Babe, can we put this on hold?"

She frowned. "What's wrong?"

"Nothing. I just got some information I was waiting on. It looks like I probably have to work a little tonight." He wanted to see if he could find out any other intel the kid had missed.

She searched his gaze and narrowed her eyes. "You're lying. What's wrong?"

Rafe's frown deepened. How did she know he was lying? He was a damn good liar. He'd spent years perfecting the ability.

"Did I do something wrong?"

What? Was she insane? "No. You didn't. You, and this, are exactly what I need. I just have to work."

She tipped her chin up. "I don't believe you. Just tell me what's going on. Does it involve me?"

Rafe clenched his jaw, and she took that as an affirmation.

"Okay, now you have to tell me."

He hated to do it, to make her think that she was going crazy. But he had to because right now, they couldn't get into it. She would worry, and she'd been through enough as it was. "Look, if you need to know something, I'll tell you."

She placed her hand on her hips and gave him a withering look. "Really? Now it's 'need to know.' I'm the little *lady*, the damsel in distress? Okay, look. I needed you to rescue me down the side of a ravine. Fair enough. But since you brought me here, I've been pulling my weight, trying not to be a burden. Not be a bother. I appreciate it. I don't want to impact your life more than I already have. But I thought things had changed with us. I thought maybe something was happening."

Rafe's frustration bubbled to the surface. "Yeah, I thought so too. But you've been damn secretive about your past, even knowing that I'm worried about your safety. I keep waiting to walk in here and find you gone."

She glowered at him. "*I* keep waiting to be kicked out. For you to tell me I've overstayed my welcome. Hell, for all I know you have a girlfriend."

Rafe threw up his hands. "Look around. Does it look like I have a girlfriend? I go to work, and I come home. Until recently, that was the extent of it. Maybe a little football on TV, pass out. Do it all again. Only lately, I've tacked on giving you three orgasms a night before you pass out to my list of things to do."

"Oh, thank you for those orgasms, but if it means I can't ask questions, if it means that I can't know what you're trying to do on my behalf, then I don't want them."

He scowled and stepped forward, crowding her. "Let's not kid ourselves. You want it." He licked his lips when her pupils dilated again. "But don't think I wasn't deadly serious when I said I would protect you."

"I never asked you to."

"When I'm done with this, we're going to pick this conversation right up where we left off."

"Yeah, some conversation. If it involves you dictating to me, then I'm not particularly interested. I think I'll just head to bed."

"The hell you will. We're not done."

The smile she gave him was evil. Then she started to strip. Sports bra first. Then yoga pants. His cerebral cortex shorted out. She didn't give him a chance to recover. Instead, she turned on her heel and strode down the hall to the bathroom.

Fuck.

13

On his first trip through the neighborhood, Rafe didn't slow down when he passed the house in question. It was a decent neighborhood with neatly manicured lawns and trees planted in rows along the sidewalks, the kind of place he could see himself living in someday. And surprise, surprise, his imagination conjured up a helpful image of Diana there with him.

Rafe would have never thought he could enjoy such simple, basic pleasures as coming home to a woman who was happy to see him. But seeing Diana was quickly becoming his favorite part of every day. She always had a smile for him that made him feel about ten feet tall.

The warmth he felt just being around her was unlike anything he'd ever experienced with a woman before.

This wasn't just desire. Desire he was familiar with. Rafe loved women and certainly hadn't been a monk in his past, but it had always been enough to spend a night with a woman and then move on. It made him feel like an asshole, but he'd never wanted anything more than that. Some people functioned better on their own, and he'd always figured that the only family he needed was Nonna, Lucia, and the gaggle of kids he'd always known his sister would one day have.

He wouldn't have described himself as lonely before. There was an uncomplicated beauty in living alone and having every part of his life regimented. Due to his years of training to be invisible, it was easier to be alone. But he couldn't deny that a part of him was awakening being around Diana. She didn't ask for much from him other than his company, and she made him feel that was a gift. He'd puzzled over it for days before realizing that she simply liked him as he was. What a revelation.

So when Rafe finally got the details from Matthias about Diana's ex-boyfriend, there was no question of how he'd handle it. When they'd met, she'd been scared and hurt, and no amount of time would erase that image from his mind. For a man like him, there was only one thing to do when someone he cared about was in danger.

Eliminate the threat.

Rafe shook his head. He couldn't kill the guy. After years being in ORUS, and to a lesser degree the FBI, it was hard to shed their *kill first, ask questions later* mentality. But he was transitioning back into a civilian. This was what he'd always wanted and what he'd bargained so hard for. He couldn't do anything to jeopardize his chance to live freely again, so he would have to step carefully.

But just because he couldn't kill the guy didn't mean he couldn't take care of the problem. By the time he was done, Corbin James would never even look askance at another woman. He'd be lucky if he wasn't pissing into a bag.

Rafe continued to drive around, making sure not to linger too long on any street until he saw what he'd been waiting for—a blue SUV parked in the driveway. Rafe smiled.

Corbin James was home from work.

He parked on the street behind the house and walked through the back neighbor's yard to a small copse of trees right behind the house. According to Matthias, Mr. James had a dog. Rafe had never had one, but the little he knew about them included how often they needed to be taken outside, which would give him the opportunity he needed. Rafe glanced at his watch and waited patiently. Ten minutes later, a man stepped out onto the back porch with a puppy on a leash.

Moving quickly, Rafe scooped up the dog, jerked the leash from James's hand, and deposited the pup inside the house, closing the door behind it. The little guy would try to protect his owner, and he'd never enjoyed the thought of hurting a defenseless animal. The dog didn't even bark, just pressed its little face against the glass, observing Rafe curiously.

"Some guard dog you've got there," he commented as he turned around.

The other man backed up, his eyes darting nervously between Rafe and the back door.

"What the hell, man? Who are you?"

Rafe punched him in the gut and then cradled him on his way down to the ground. "I'm the guy who is going to kick your ass."

Corbin wheezed, in too much pain to even scream. Rafe had hit him right in the lung, so he wouldn't be breathing normally for a while. Plenty of time for them to have a talk.

Well, for Rafe to talk and for Corbin to listen.

"Get away, help!" The soft scream was cut off when Rafe grabbed him by the throat. He enjoyed the man's look of terror. Was that how Diana had felt when this asshole had kicked her in the ribs? Had he stalked her around this house, letting her feel the terror of being hunted before he'd hurt her? The thought of her being scared and helpless enraged him, and his hand tightened around the other man's throat. The gurgling below him was the only thing that prompted him to loosen his grip.

Don't kill him.

"Is that her dog?" Rafe glanced back at the house as the thought occurred to him. That seemed like the kind of thing that Diana would have talked about. She was such a gentle spirit—he couldn't imagine her leaving a puppy behind easily.

"Who? That's my dog. Just got him. I'm sorry I forgot to pooper-scoop yesterday!"

Rafe scowled. "Do I look like I'm from the fucking homeowners' association? I don't care about your dog's poop. I'm here because of Diana."

Corbin dragged in a greedy breath as soon as Rafe's grip relaxed a bit. "Who? Man, I don't know what you're talking about. I just came home to walk my dog."

"You don't know who I'm talking about? You don't remember kicking Diana so hard a few weeks ago that you bruised her ribs?"

Rafe waited for the inevitable sniveling and excuses. When they didn't come, he looked down into the man's confused expression.

"Diana who? Man, I don't even know who that is!"

"Of course you don't."

Corbin shook his head and then winced. He put a hand to his throat where purple bruises from Rafe's fingers were already forming.

These assholes never took responsibility for their actions. He'd seen this sort of thing back in his neighborhood, but he'd been too young to do much to help back then. Once he'd started training Noah, they'd been happy to use their skills to help those who couldn't help themselves.

Noah had kept up the practice when he started his own security firm, something that made Rafe proud. Even after he'd been out of Noah's life, the things he'd instilled in the kid had stuck and guided him into becoming the kind of man that Rafe had always known he could be. It was good to see that something he'd done had turned out right.

Corbin used his inattention to back away, crab walking backward until he bumped into the small table on the patio. "Just take my wallet. I have a lot of cash in there!"

Rafe kicked one of the chairs out of his way. "I don't want money. What I want is to make sure you never hurt Diana or any other woman again."

Corbin tripped over his own feet trying to get away.

Rafe caught him by the back of the shirt and yanked him back.

"Diana Renquist. Doesn't ring any bells, right? Let me guess, you conveniently forget every woman after you use her as a punching bag."

Corbin held up his hands. "Punching bag? Man, do I look like I would punch anyone?"

Rafe paused, looking at the man's long, thin, clearly manicured fingers. Was that— Wait, was that nail polish? The dude had hands that looked like they belonged in a lotion commercial, pale and smooth. Although that didn't mean anything. There were plenty of abusive men who put on an elegant façade in public while living their lives as monsters at night.

"Wait, Renquist? You mean the chick who lived here before me?"

"Huh?" Rafe loosened his grip slightly.

The other man gulped. "Yeah. There was some lady with that name who lived here before me. I still get her mail sometimes."

Rafe had a long history of dealing with liars, which was how he knew that Corbin James was very likely telling the truth. But that meant that along the way, he'd gotten something very wrong.

But then, who was she running from? And who the hell had hurt her? Had she not told him because she feared something like this would happen? Feared what he would do?

He'd almost killed this guy. Based on what? An overheard conversation and a hunch?

It's no wonder she doesn't trust you with the whole story.

WHEN DIANA WALKED down the sidewalk to reach Charisse's house, she found her friend waiting for her at the door.

After a quick hug, Diana followed her inside. There was a soft, nubby throw blanket over the back of the couch and a colorful painting on the wall that she'd never seen before.

"I see you've made a few changes since I've been gone."

Charisse harrumphed. "You would have known that if you'd come by more often."

Diana laughed. "I know, I'm sorry. I've been a crap friend. I just… I don't want to risk being followed."

"No, you haven't. You've been dealing with some stuff. I get that." Charisse shooed her toward the sofa and then came back with two cans of cold soda. "Besides, you're here now, even if I don't agree with the reason why."

Diana glanced at her from the corner of her eye. "Does that mean you got it?"

"Hell yeah, I got it. I told you I had a hookup. My brother is friends with the guy who coded this one. It'll work on any digital safe. You just have to give it enough time to do the job."

That was the trick, wasn't it? Finding enough time without interruption to let the safe decoder work. Rafe left her in the apartment alone now, but it was never more than a few hours. What if that wasn't enough time? With the kind of encryption he had on that safe, it could take longer.

"I'll find a way," Diana muttered. "This is the only option I really have."

"Or you could stop this whole thing and get out before that dude finds out what you're up to." Charisse ignored the withering glance Diana gave her. "I'm serious. You've been lucky so far that nothing has gone wrong. Please, think this through before you get in too deep."

Diana didn't say anything. What could she say? No matter how she phrased things, there was no way to explain to her friend that she was already in too deep and there was no going back now. She needed to know the truth. Understanding the events of the worst day of her life was the only way she'd ever have any kind of closure. The confusing feelings she had for Rafe wouldn't go away until she could answer the questions she had.

"Oh shit. It's already too late, isn't it?" Charisse shook her head and set her soda can down on the coffee table. "What the hell are you doing?"

"I have no idea," Diana whispered.

Charisse sighed. "I knew this was a bad idea."

They sat in silence for a while. Finally Diana leaned over and rested her head on Charisse's shoulder. She closed her eyes, letting herself process for the first time what would happen once she was confronted with the evidence of what Rafe had done. It was one thing to suspect that Rafe had killed her father so he could steal the Jewel of the Sea, but another to see the evidence in front of her face.

What then?

"You certainly know how to keep things interesting, don't you?" Charisse finally chuckled.

"That's me. Never boring." Her voice sounded as despondent as she felt.

Charisse pulled back, forcing Diana to sit up straight. "Tell me the truth. You have it bad for this guy, don't you?"

With it stated so plainly, Diana couldn't do anything but nod helplessly.

"And once you have the diamond back? Or at least find out who he sold it to?"

Diana shivered. "I don't know, Char. These past few weeks with him have been intense. Nothing is what I thought it would be, least of all him. It's surreal."

Charisse grabbed her hands. "It's not surreal. Unfortunately, this whole situation is very, very real. And he will really kill you if he finds out that you've been plotting against him this whole time. You're sleeping with him now. It's just terrifying to think of all the ways he can hurt you. I'm worried."

Diana fought the urge to pull away. Her friend was just looking out for her and trying to be the voice of reason in an unreasonable situation. But that didn't make what she was saying any easier to hear.

"I know. Believe me. This is real to me. My body wants him, I don't deny that, but my brain knows the deal. The only important thing is getting revenge for my father and recovering my mother's legacy. I haven't lost sight of that."

A loud sigh told her that her friend wasn't completely convinced, but one of the valuable things about being friends with someone for so long was knowing they'd be there for you anyway.

"Okay. You know I'm here for you if you ever need to

talk." Charisse patted her hand. "Wait here while I get your stuff."

Diana watched as she left the room. She looked around curiously. The furniture was sturdy, and everything was in a shade of beige. Despite that, Charisse had decorated with pops of color here and there that kept things cheerful. You could see her friend's personality all over the room from the daisies in a vase in the center of the table to the piles of books on every surface mixed in with her kids' toys. Eclectic but fun.

Would she ever have that? The opportunity to put her stamp somewhere and carve out a space that was purely her own? She'd spent so much time pursuing justice that now she wasn't sure what she'd do if she got it. Who was she if she wasn't avenging her father?

It had been a long time since she'd thought about that.

"Okay, here it is. Use with caution." Charisse appeared at the end of the couch, holding a small box with a digital face, and the black bag Diana had left in her long-term hotel room weeks ago. "I hope I got the right bag."

Diana held the bag in her lap and unzipped it. It contained her laptop, a charger, money, and her real identification. "This is exactly what I needed. Thank you for getting this for me. I didn't want to take a chance in case Rafe has been watching me."

Charisse held out the small box. "This is the decoder. Put it over the keypad and then let it run. It could take anywhere from one to five hours."

"Got it." Diana stood and accepted the device gratefully. "Thanks again, Char. It means a lot, especially since I know you don't agree with any of this."

"That's what friends are for, right? Besides, it's not that I don't agree with it. I want you to get your revenge. I just want to make sure that you don't end up getting played... or worse."

CHARISSE'S WORDS stayed with her the whole way home. Was that what was happening? Was she getting played?

Diana turned the phrase over and over in her mind as she looked out the windows of the taxi at the streets of New York. She was here, finally, and doing what she'd always dreamed of. Bringing her father's murderer to justice for the pain and devastation he'd caused.

The idea that she was failing at something she'd spent so much of her life dreaming about was disturbing.

"Hey, lady. You gettin' out or what?" The cabbie's

voice broke into her thoughts, and Diana scrambled to pull some money out of her pocket. Even that made her think of Rafe since it was no doubt some of the money he'd given her.

That went for the clothes she was wearing and the shoes on her feet. All provided by Rafe. She thrust the money over the seat to the cabbie and climbed out, suddenly wanting nothing more than to strip it all off. To be free and clear of any reminder of why she was here. But she couldn't do that. He'd be back any minute, and she needed to be there so she didn't have to answer any questions about where she'd been. The whole thing was a delicate balancing act of lies, and she was suddenly exhausted from the performance. But giving up now would mean giving up on justice for her father.

He deserved better than that.

But what about what you deserve? Wouldn't he have wanted more for you than this?

It startled her to realize that her father probably wouldn't have wanted her to move on. He'd been big on vendettas. She'd seen his scathing temper in action more than a few times. He'd have been proud of her for dedicating her life to evening a score.

Which didn't make her feel any better.

She'd deliberately given the cabbie an address down the street from Rafe's building. If anyone asked around, there would be no record of a cab dropping off a woman at his building. But as she walked down the street, she wished she'd picked a closer drop-off point. A man walking in the opposite direction slowed down and gave a wolf whistle as she passed.

When she didn't respond, she heard the muttered "Bitch," but she didn't stop walking.

Then she heard the footsteps.

She slowed, and the footsteps slowed as well. When she sped up, they matched pace. Furious, she spun around to confront the guy and then... faced an empty street. There was no one there except for the homeless man she'd just passed, and he hadn't moved.

"Damn it. Now I'm just getting paranoid."

But she knew from experience that being paranoid could sometimes save your life.

She hurried the rest of the way, breathing a sigh of relief when Rafe's building loomed ahead. Her skin was still prickling like someone was watching, but at this point she couldn't tell what was real and what was in her head. But she kept her eyes open and alert as she entered the building and rode the elevator up to Rafe's floor.

"Rafe? Hello?"

No answer. Mentally she cheered because it meant she still had time. Even though Charisse had said to expect it to take hours, there was nothing wrong with giving it a go now. Maybe she'd get lucky and it would work right away. Then she'd have the answers she needed and could put all this needless speculation to rest.

Diana wasted no time, heading straight for Rafe's office. She pressed the painting and waited as the panel slid open. Then she placed the decoder over the keypad on the safe. With one eye on the door, she watched as numbers flashed across the screen.

It's running through combinations, she realized with fascination. The decoder was literally going to try every combination possible until it found the right one. No wonder it could take hours.

Her shoulders sagged. It was too risky to try this now. Rafe could come home at any minute, and she'd have no reasonable explanation for why she was in his office. So it would make more sense to wait until he had another call for a job. His security work usually took him away from the apartment for hours at a time.

Or she could make the time. Her gut knotted up at the thought. Rafe had knocked over the glass of wine that she'd laced last time. But that didn't mean she couldn't try again. Maybe she'd hide it in food this time. He'd never know. Then she'd have all the time she needed.

And this could finally be over.

But could she do it? Diana took the decoder off and closed the panel hiding the safe. She wasn't sure she had too many other alternatives outside of waiting for him to leave on his own. Considering how weird his schedule was, it could be days or weeks until he was called out on another job. That wasn't that long in the grand scheme of things, but it was still longer than necessary.

She'd been here for weeks and was only getting more and more comfortable. It was time she got serious again.

14

Diana used her phone and checked Rafe's location. He was almost home. The real question was whether or not she could go through with it. She glanced down at the pill in her hand. What the hell was wrong with her? She'd come this far. This pill, it wasn't supposed to hurt him... much. It was like sodium pentothal. She ignored the fact that most governments considered its use torture. And this... she'd been told that these pills might have side effects similar to MDMA. Could she use it on him?

It would just get her the truth. Get her what she needed, and then she could go before she sank in even deeper with him.

You're an idiot for letting him get so close.

Shit. She *was* an idiot. She didn't have to be told

twice. With every touch of his, or glance, or caress, her armor slipped.

Without even trying, he'd found the chinks. The man he pretended to be had slid in under her skin, making a home there, infesting her brain, making it impossible to think straight.

You sure your brain is what he infested?

He had killed her father. She could never forgive that even if this new version of him seemed like a good man. She couldn't risk believing it.

He's a killer. Remember that.

She stared down at the pill. Maybe Charisse was right. Maybe she'd sunk too deep. Maybe she was in way over her head.

Stop it. Because of him, your father is no longer here.

Her phone alerted her that Rafe was essentially outside the door. She glanced at the little white pill again. Could she do it? Could she hurt him?

Her hands shook. She knew the answer before she even asked it. She couldn't. *Because you're an idiot, and you're falling for him.*

Even though she knew everything he showed her was a lie, her hands still trembled as she held the little pill.

Despite all the things she said to herself, she knew it was true. She was screwed. She'd gone ahead and fallen in love with the mark. She put the pill back in the bottle and placed the cap on it before tossing it back into her purse.

If she couldn't see this through, her only option was to leave him. And that thought hurt more than anything.

When he walked in the door, she instantly knew something was wrong.

"Hey," she said warily, then poured him a glass of wine.

He smiled, but it didn't reach his eyes. That was the smile he gave people so they wouldn't look too closely. Maybe someone who'd never seen his real one wouldn't know the difference, but it hit her like a ton of bricks. He was hiding something from her. Her other clue something was horribly wrong was the way he took the glass from her and drained it.

She took the glass and set it on the coffee table. "Is everything okay? How was work?"

Rafe hung his coat in the front closet before sitting on the couch. He let out a little sigh when he sat that told her he was tired. That really confirmed her suspicion. The man had unbelievable stamina. She blushed, thinking of how many ways he'd proven that to her. It would take more than just a stressful day to make Rafe tired. Then he turned his head, and she saw the scratch on the side of his neck. Her eyes narrowed as she scanned him from head to toe.

She took one of his hands and gasped. "You got in a fight?"

Rafe sighed and stopped struggling. "Not exactly."

Something about the way he said it made her stomach pitch. She thought about all the times he'd asked her who had hurt her over the past weeks and his insistence that he'd make it right for her, and her stomach sank.

"Rafe, what did you do?" she whispered.

He glanced over at her. "You'll be safe now. No one's going to hurt you."

Oh God. Diana closed her eyes and swallowed the bitter tang of guilt. He'd found the poor guy she'd pretended was her ex-boyfriend, and if the state of his knuckles was any indication, he'd probably beaten the guy to a pulp.

"You shouldn't have done that." That was the understatement of the century. He was trying to defend her nonexistent honor and had almost taken out some poor guy who had nothing to do with anything. Diana felt like she was drowning under the weight of all the lies between them.

"You're mine, and I take care of what's mine. You make me feel things, Diana." He dipped his mouth to hers, and as soon as their tongues met, electricity coursed through her body.

She reminded herself of the million reasons why they shouldn't do this. At the core, he was a killer and she was a liar. He could have killed that guy today based on her lies. There was just too much wrong between them, secrets and lies and agendas. But somehow when they were together, it all fell away and none of it seemed like it mattered.

But it did. People were getting hurt because of their mistakes.

Diana placed her fingertips against his mouth, trying to stop things before they spun out of control. She had a tendency to lose track of time and space when she was in his arms. But she needed to make sure some poor guy hadn't just died because of her.

"Rafe. Tell me what happened."

By the mulish expression on his face, she thought he wasn't going to answer, but then she poked him in the side.

"I paid a visit to that asshole who hurt you."

Shit, shit, shit. What had he told Rafe? She swallowed. "Is he still alive?" Her heart squeezed.

Rafe frowned. "Yes. I wouldn't—" He lowered his voice to a whisper. "I don't— That's not the kind of man I want to be."

"What kind of man do you want to be then?" Diana kissed his bruised knuckles. Could he be distracted from this conversation?

"A just one. I do what's necessary to protect the innocent." He glanced down at his hands. "As it stands, I was barely able to control myself. And that makes me sick."

"Rafe," she whispered. "You didn't have to do that."

"I thought I did. When I went there, I wanted to make sure he understood that the things we do have consequences. I was his consequence. After all, he'd hurt what was mine. That was why I went there. But I realized that I didn't belong there."

Hell. He knew. He had to know.

"I'm yours?" Even though he'd said it before, it had felt more like the product of high emotions and rushing testosterone. Men said all kinds of things in the moment that they didn't actually mean. But this was different.

"How could you not know how I feel about you?" Rafe dragged her forward and kissed her again. On a shocked breath, she opened for him again. He angled his head to deepen the kiss. When he touched his tongue to hers, she stilled and backed away, flattening a hand against his chest.

"You can tell me anything. You know that, right? Diana—"

"Wait. I just need a minute to breathe." She pushed

her hair away from her face and tried to take a breath. She battled conflicting emotions—worry over what Rafe had done on her behalf and guilt at her own deception. She was caught up in a web of lies and didn't know how to untangle herself. What the hell had she done to his life?

There were so many questions and no answers, and the swirl of confusion was making her head hurt. But for the first time in her life, she felt alive. Like she was doing more than just existing from one day to the next.

Whether it was right or wrong, she couldn't resist one more chance to feel alive in Rafe's arms. For the rest of her days, she doubted she'd ever feel like this again.

If she had been unsure about leaving him before, now it was even clearer why she needed to. Despite everything she knew, she loved him. And she couldn't keep doing this to either of them. She needed to leave before she destroyed them both.

She swiped a tear off her cheek. "I didn't want this, Rafe."

"Baby, don't cry. Please don't be scared. I would never hurt you."

Rafe shifted slightly, looking as wrecked as she felt. This back-and-forth was taking a toll on both of them.

"I know."

She cut him off by tugging him to her and fusing

their lips together. He didn't need further invitation and dragged her onto his lap so she straddled him, her dress shifting up to expose her thighs.

RAFE SHOULD HAVE KNOWN this was too good to be true. All he wanted was to sink into Diana, make her come a handful of times, and hold her to sleep. That would be better than any aspirin.

But just as she hiked up her skirt, there was a knock at the door. Fuck that, he could ignore it. He slid his lips over Diana's, wanting to get lost in them.

"Rafe, don't you think you should get that?"

"Nope. Remember the last time I opened the door? Matthias cock-blocked me. I'm not taking that chance again."

She laughed even as she started to slide off his lap. Reflexively, Rafe tried to hold on to her. Literally and figuratively. She was here, present with him, but in the past few days, he'd started to feel like she was pulling away. Like she was trying to run. Was she scared of him?

Can you blame her?

Diana kissed him softly on the lips. "You get it, get rid of whoever it is, and then come to bed."

All his dick heard was *bed*. But he couldn't really

blame the guy. "Fine, but get naked. I'm not feeling particularly patient."

She only chuckled as she sashayed down the hall.

He was in no fucking mood, so if it was Matthias again just to fuck with him, he was going to kill the kid. He scowled when he checked the monitor. Shit. What the hell was *she* doing here?

He yanked the door open and scowled. "Emilie."

"Rafe, glad I caught you at home," Emilie said with a sunny smile in her barely discernable French accent. She leaned against the doorjamb with a stack of files in one arm and a case of beer in the other. "I figured we could talk. You know, unofficially. I could use your help. I'm not interrupting anything, am I?"

Rafe frowned. "Emilie? What are you doing here?" No one ever came to his place. He wasn't the kind of guy who invited company over for dinner parties. Hell, most of the guys from Blake Security, outside of Matthias and Noah, had never been here. *Though, you should probably change that.*

He'd learned that from his time in ORUS. Never bring anyone to a place you considered yours. If he wanted to talk to anyone from work, they did it in the office or they met somewhere. And there hadn't been any women worth bringing back since he'd performed his little resurrection. He took whoever he met back to their place or to a hotel.

But Diana was the exception.

He'd never thought of that as a lonely existence until now. Rafe did a quick sweep of the hallway and the floor-to-ceiling glass windows that allowed a view to the street.

Everything looked normal, but the fine hairs on the back of his neck stood at attention. Why was she here? And if this was official, why hadn't Alan called him in to talk?

She held up the six-pack. "I brought beer. Isn't that what you Americans bring over to someone's house? Beer? I personally prefer a nice bottle of wine, but I'll just assume that you have some." She winked. "Call it wishful thinking. I can't stand beer. But, nevertheless, I thought I would bring some over and we could go over these files. I have so many questions about the Vandergraffs."

Rafe didn't budge from the door. He didn't know how Emilie had known about his place, but he didn't like her showing up here unannounced. "Again, what are you doing *here*?"

She shrugged. "I had a friend dig deep through a pile of shell companies. I figured you'd buy under an alias. Very clever, but then you've always been clever."

He growled.

There was a flicker of awareness in her green eyes. "Would you relax? I just feel like there's something missing from the whole scenario. That's how I am. Like a dog with a bone. I just can't let it go when something doesn't feel right. So I just wanted to go over everything with you again in case you missed anything."

He scowled. If there was ever a bad decision to regret, it was Emilie. It was ever having anything to do with her. One night in Germany, after one too many, there'd been drunken almost-sex. But he'd gotten a call about a mission so he'd left... and never called. A year later, still pissed, she'd lied to an asset of his. That asset had died on her watch.

"Just because I'm paranoid doesn't mean someone's not out to get me."

She leaned against the doorjamb, tilting her head so that her auburn hair cascaded over one shoulder. "Come on, you going to let me in or what?" There was a shuffling behind Rafe, and before he could turn, Emilie poked her head around, peeking into the living room.

Diana said, "Sorry to interrupt, but the hot water is off for some reason, Rafe."

He frowned, then remembered the notice posted in the elevator about the pipe updates. "The water heater button is under the sink in the vanity. It's a backup system."

"Okay, thanks. Sorry again," she murmured before scooting off.

"Oh gosh, I have interrupted something. It wasn't something important, was it?"

For a long moment, Rafe considered how to answer that. Yes, she was damn well interrupting. And yes, he also had a distinct feeling that she knew that. What was she playing at? What did she really want from him? "This isn't the best time, Emilie."

But Emilie wasn't having any of that. She pushed past him and stepped into the living room as if she owned the place. At the very least as if she'd been there before, showing the confidence of a woman who was not used to being turned down, not used to people telling her no.

"I like your place, Rafe. Fancy."

He ground his teeth. "Thank you. Why don't you come right on in," he muttered under his breath.

Emilie grinned. "I guess I will." She set the files on the coffee table. Rafe shut the door behind her and followed her into the living room. He wasn't ready to make introductions, but it turned out he didn't need to worry about that. Diana was already down the hall. He prayed she was in his room.

He shoved his hands in his pockets. "Look, Emilie, this isn't a good time. I was in the middle of—"

She beamed a smile at him. "You know what, I did have a little look at your file. I know you're not married. According to the bureau, you haven't had a long-term girlfriend in a while. So I guess Little Miss Blondie is new. We're colleagues. No reason you can't be hospitable. I know you have a new life now. Or should I say old, new life. Everything old is new again. But you have loose ends that need tying up."

Rafe crossed his arms. "Emilie, my relationships are none of your business. While I do appreciate your stopping by, I also have other things I need to do. Remember, I'm a civilian now. And quite frankly, none of this is my problem anymore."

It was the first time he'd seen Emilie's smile falter.

"I guess I'm intruding. But I really do have some questions about the Vandergraffs. The file said the daughter was supposed to be with her friends that night. But when we followed up, that friend said she wasn't there. So where did the girl go? What luck she wasn't in the house when the hit went down."

Rafe gritted his teeth. "If she had been, I would have reported it."

She smiled and nodded. But he could tell from her eyes that she didn't believe him. "Of course *you* would've." She nodded toward the back rooms. "I guess your girlfriend is waiting on you?" Emilie's eyes narrowed toward the back hall.

"Yes. She is. So you'd better go."

"Fair enough. I'll save our sleuthing for the office then. As the details of this case are classified, it's not wise to discuss it where someone else might overhear. I'll call Alan to set something up."

"That's probably for the best. Besides"—he shrugged—"I've given you all the details I have of that night."

"Well, it's always a good idea to double-check. I suppose I'll let you get back to your *guest*."

What was she playing at? Why was she really here? She couldn't think that he'd possibly be interested after everything that had happened before.

"Perfect. I look forward to a more official meeting."

She smiled up at him. "You go ahead and enjoy that beer though. Hope you and your *guest* enjoy the night."

Rafe showed her the door and deliberately avoided her attempt to brush up against him. "I'll be seeing you, Emilie."

"That you will, Rafe DeMarco."

After Rafe locked up and reset the security alarms, he pinched the bridge of his nose, his headache having become more prominent.

That's what happens when you live a life of lies. They weigh on you.

In the kitchen, he found just what he needed on the counter. It looked like it had fallen out of Diana's purse.

Picking up the bottle of aspirin, he took two. He'd carved a new life for himself. He was a new man now. The past was the past. Dredging up that old file would just drag him back to a place he never wanted to go again.

He was not that man. He wasn't. And he resented Emilie trying to remind him of who he used to be. His future was down the hall and uptown in a glass penthouse. *Family*. He'd forgotten how important they were.

He was never going to be out in the cold again.

15

Rafe stood in the kitchen for a few minutes, too wound up by Emilie's visit to pretend. Diana would want to know what was wrong and there was nothing he could tell her. She didn't know about his past and how he was trying to reinvent himself. With her, he'd been able to start fresh, and he didn't have to drag any of that shit into what he had with her.

He liked that what he had with her was pure. Untouched.

Gradually his thoughts turned back to where they'd left off, and he imagined her naked and wet in his bed. His erection sprang up immediately, and he followed it like a beacon to the room where Diana reclined on the bed. All he could see was soft skin, pink lips, and a smile.

At the sight of her, he felt a punch of lust so strong it almost took him to his knees. He climbed onto the bed and over her. Dimly, he realized that he was going too fast. Being too rough. But suddenly all he could think about was her—her smell, her taste, being inside her.

"Need to feel you," he rasped before burying his face in her neck and breathing deep.

Diana scratched her nails through his hair, and a wave of lust drowned out rational thinking. He cupped her breast and groaned as the soft, plump globe filled his hand. *God.*

Every time she touched him, electricity arced between them. A woman's touch had never affected him like this. What they had was pure fire.

Shifting off the bed, he yanked off his jeans, and her eyes focused on his thick erection.

Her eyes on his flesh only made him harder.

Rafe climbed back over her and placed open-mouthed kisses along her jawline, the column of her throat, her collarbone. When he dipped to kiss her breasts again, she moaned just before his lips covered the pointed tip. With his other hand, he teased the other nipple until she whimpered. Releasing her nipple, Rafe continued the path of hot kisses down her stomach, past her belly button.

Rafe settled between her thighs and gave a long,

leisurely lick of her pussy. Diana dug her hands into his hair, but he didn't stop the expert strokes of his tongue except to occasionally nip and suck on her flesh.

Diana shuddered and cried out.

His deft thumbs separated her flesh slowly. He slid a finger into her and murmured against her flesh. "C'mon sweetheart. Come for me."

In an instant, she exploded. Her cries and whimpers were so fucking arousing that Rafe figured his dick could pound through concrete by now. He grimaced and gripped his erection, trying to calm down. What the hell was wrong with him? He'd never had any issues with control before, but he legitimately felt like he might come at any moment.

"What's wrong?" Diana murmured. She trailed her hand down his chest, and he drew in a ragged breath when she found what she sought.

"Oh, fuck, Diana." His hips bucked, pushing his straining erection into her hand.

She trailed hot, openmouthed kisses along the column of his throat and when she found his nipple, his hips bucked again. With her thumb, she stroked the soft round head of his length, spreading the moisture that had leaked.

Hovering her lips over his erect nipple, she whispered, "Is something wrong, Rafe?"

Something that sounded like a strangled moan tore from his chest, and he dug his hands into the sheets.

"I'll take that as a no." Diana brushed her lips over his taut nipple and chuckled at the groan that tore from his throat.

He bucked again, digging a hand into her hair, gently tugging her head back. "I swear to God, Diana—"

She ignored him, instead grazing his nipple and pumping his erection again.

Before she could move, he had her flat on her back and her hands locked above her head, restrained with one of his.

"Rafe?" She struggled slightly, and he realized all at once how tight he'd been holding her. He sat back and ran his hands through his hair. He needed to slow down, but he wasn't sure he could. His body was reacting like he'd been away from her for years instead of minutes.

Maybe this was what it was like when you were with someone you cared about?

Rafe reached over to the nightstand and grabbed a condom. Rolling away, he sheathed himself before settling back between her thighs. He kissed her deep, and Diana widened her legs to accommodate him. His erection nudged her, and she moaned as he sank inside.

He dropped his forehead to hers, retreated an inch,

then pressed forward again until he was fully seated inside her. Her name on his lips sounded reverent.

Her gaze met his, and immediately none of it mattered anymore. In this moment, everything was perfect. She felt perfect.

The corners of his lips tipped into a lopsided smile as he retreated and sank back in. Diana clamped her legs around his hips, and he muttered curses under his breath. When she pulled him to her for a kiss, he growled low in his throat.

Diana nipped his lower lip with her teeth, and he scooped his hands under her ass, lifting her hips to his. The new angle had her sobbing at the pleasure. Only when she murmured his name on a sigh did he stroke into her a final time, then cry out her name on his climax.

DIANA'S BREATH lodged in her throat as Rafe slid his tongue over hers again. After three orgasms back-to-back, he showed no signs of slowing down. The man had crazy stamina, she knew that, but this was unlike anything she'd ever seen.

He was kissing her like he was afraid she'd disappear if he let go. She'd never been the center of a man's attention like this before.

She slipped her hands over Rafe's torso, skimming over rippled abdominal muscles and the hard planes of his chest. The sounds he made at her touch were more like pain than pleasure, but when she paused, he canted his hips, bringing the hot, hard length of him directly against her heat again.

"Again. Already?" she squeaked.

To hold on and attempt some level of control, she slid her fingers into the thick, soft curls at his nape and gently tugged. With a moan, he smoothed a hand down her back to the curve of her ass and tucked her closer to his body. She rolled her hips into his, and Rafe tore his mouth from hers with a harsh curse.

"Diana, you're addictive. I can't stop."

She trembled in his arms. "Then don't."

Diana shivered as Rafe kissed her softly before shifting her so her head was closer to the headboard. He then settled his body between her legs, tracing a path of kisses from her lips to her jaw, to the sensitive hollow between her neck and her ear. Slowly, he brushed kisses over her belly, and Diana held her breath.

Leaning down, he breathed soft kisses on first one, then the other nipple, each responding to his caress by instantly budding into hard little peaks. Focusing his attention on one, he drew the dark bud into his mouth, taking greedy tugs while his thumb teased the other.

Diana bucked, and her back bowed as pleasure reverberated through her body.

"Yes, I need more. I can't stop." Rafe panted hard.

That's when she noticed how flushed his cheeks were. He was bright red, like he'd just run a marathon.

"Are you okay? You're all red."

He lifted his head. "I'm not surprised. I feel like I'm on fire. You drive me crazy, you know that?"

Sure fingers slid through her lips, seeking her center. Rafe met her gaze as he found his quarry. Dark eyes, wild with lust, gazed at her, watching her reaction as his questing finger found the center of her torment.

She cried out as he gently sank into her. Rafe held perfectly still except for his questing finger, gently exploring and retreating, occasionally detouring to swirl around her clit but always returning to delve just a little deeper inside her.

"Jesus, you are so tight. So hot..." He bit his bottom lip as he sank in with two fingers and his thumb traced circles on her clit.

Molten heat spread through her body. She parted her legs to give him even better access to her folds. "Rafe..."

Instead of coaxing a response from her, he

demanded one, and her body gave him what he wanted. His thigh wedged between her legs, bringing him in contact with her throbbing clit. She could feel the heat and hardness of his leg muscles and the friction he applied to her sweet spot. Her hips gave an involuntary jerk, and he gave her a satisfied grunt.

He left a trail of buzzing nerve endings in his wake as his hand traveled up her belly, then her ribs to her breast. His lips slid back over hers as his thumb skimmed the underside of her breast. Another shot of lust hit her hard, and she rocked her hips on his thigh. When he did it again, Diana threw her head back.

He trailed kisses along her jawline, then dipped his head farther to her neck. He traced a thumb over her nipple and she cried out. Moisture and heat rushed to her center, and the building need tipped her close to the edge of ecstasy. It wouldn't take much. Just one more stroke from his deft fingers, maybe two.

"Jesus, you are so beautiful," he whispered.

"Rafe..."

Suddenly his fingers slid away. Diana opened her eyes to find him slumped over, his eyes closed.

"Oh my God. Rafe?"

His eyes opened instantly. "Hmm?" His eyes latched on to her bare breasts and he smiled. "You're so beautiful."

She gasped. "What just happened? Are you sick?"

His brow furrowed. "No, I'm fine now. I took the aspirin in your purse."

Diana's mouth fell open as his eyes closed again. Holy shit. He'd drugged himself! Guilt assailed her as she pressed a hand against his forehead.

Well, that definitely explained his out-of-control libido tonight. But she hadn't expected him to just conk out all of a sudden either.

As she watched him sleep, dread crept through her system. If she'd been waiting for a sign, there would never be a clearer one than this. Rafe would be out for hours.

This was her chance.

DIANA GENTLY MOVED over the mattress, grabbing Rafe's shirt from the floor and pulling it over her head. Everything from her muscles to her soft center ached from the many times they'd made love. But the thing that hurt the most was her heart. Pain sliced through the beating organ. She knew she didn't have a choice, but the thought of leaving him... of hurting him... it still pained her. What would he think? How would he feel when she left him?

Too late to worry about that. Now it's time to move. Before he wakes up.

If she assumed he'd taken two since he thought they were aspirin, he'd be out all night. But she still couldn't afford to waste any of that time. What if the decoder needed all that time to work?

At the threshold of the room, she looked back at his prone form on the bed. Rafe had rolled to his side, his muscular body looking like a sculpture in the soft light from the window. Her hands had been over every inch of that magnificent form, and she was still tempted to go back for more. After how insatiable he'd been, she should have been tired. But there was no such thing as *too* much Rafe. The man was more than a snack—he was a full buffet.

She knew how much Rafe wanted her when it was just the two of them, but add in a dose of whatever was in the pills and the effects were stratospheric.

He'd been Rafe, but he wasn't as gentle as he usually was with her. The desperation in him was evident, in the way he'd gripped her, the grit of his teeth when he slid inside her. All night he'd been on the razor's edge of tension. And he'd made love to her with a desperation unlike anything she'd seen or felt before.

Maybe he knew you were leaving.

A part of her liked it. Another part of her, the saner

part, was worried about how much he held back. He did that for her. Oh yes, they'd made love before. And it was so intense it made her skin burn. But he'd been deliberately gentle with her before. Refusing to let go of control. Tonight there was no more control, and she realized she'd been looking for that.

Up until she'd come here, her life had been so rigid and mapped out. She liked the sense of freedom she felt with Rafe. *Well, you won't have any freedom if you stay here. Get moving.*

She shoved aside her guilt and padded down the hall to her room to get dressed. With stark efficiency, she dragged on underwear, yoga pants, and a long-sleeved T-shirt, then a pair of socks.

Five minutes later, she was in his office, pushing the painting to access the safe. She placed the decoder over the keypad and turned it on.

She went back to her room and quietly started packing, checking on the decoder every fifteen minutes or so. After the first hour, she went to the kitchen and started packing food. Once she was gone, she planned to hunker down in her hotel room and figure out her next steps.

Her heart skipped a beat at the thought. What if this was it? In the next hour or so, she could be holding the Jewel of the Sea in her hands. She'd spent so long dreaming about recovering her legacy that the thought of being this close was paralyzing.

Let's not get ahead of ourselves. The decoder might not even work.

She crept down the hallway toward the office and pushed open the door. Then she gasped.

It was finished. All she has to do was turn the handle.

You do this, there's no going back. You don't get to keep him. You don't get to pretend that Diana and Rafe could have been together.

That thought kept her frozen in position for way too long. She *wanted* to be with him. She *wanted* to stay. She *wanted* to feel his not-so-gentle kiss on her lips. She *wanted* to make him lose control again, but next time without the benefit of drugs. She wanted him to be that desperate for her. *The only thing he'll feel now is desperation to catch you.*

No. It was too late for all that. She'd made her bed before she ever came here. Gripping the brushed-nickel handle, she turned it down. The safe gave way with no audible sound. The door cleared to reveal a few folders, several stacks of cash and a thumb drive.

No diamond.

And instead of disappointment, Diana felt a brief flash of joy that it wasn't there.

When her thoughts stopped swirling, she reached out and took everything out of the safe. A few bundles of cash. A stack of folders. A flash drive.

She grabbed the tiny laptop Charisse had retrieved for her. She needed to know what was on that drive.

There was just one problem. She wanted Rafe to be the man she'd gotten to know over these past few weeks, not the killer she'd been told he was. Either way, she was going to have to hurt him, and there was no way she was going to get to keep him.

16

She shoved the flash drive inside. The command prompt told her it would take three minutes to decrypt the files, and she wasted no time.

She took the laptop back to her room and set it on the bed. Then she opened the closet to look for something to put her things in, finally settling on a small duffel bag. She'd gathered everything together, but she couldn't very well carry it all in a shopping bag. Still, she hesitated before taking it, but she knew what she had to do. Funny that after everything she'd done to him, she paused at the thought of stealing his duffel bag.

He's not going to care about the bag once he realizes what you've done. The annoying little voice in the back of her mind just wouldn't stop pointing out the obvious.

While the files were still opening, she packed the rest of her things. She had to be ready to move. Rafe wouldn't sleep forever, and she was already pushing it. Maybe part of her was hoping he'd wake early and stop her from leaving. He'd tell her that he didn't care who she was or that she'd been plotting against him from the start, that he loved her anyway and they could take on the world together.

Yeah, right.

But even as she sneered at the overly sappy thought, her heart banged a mournful beat in her chest. She could deny it all she wanted, but there would always be a part of her that wished that scenario could be real. Her stomach clenched.

She should stop the pretending. He'd hate her in mere hours.

By the time she finished shoving her clothes in the bag and had swiped all her toiletries from the bathroom sink as well, the computer was done. She clicked on the program to see just what Rafe had deemed important enough to keep under lock and key.

She understood why it had taken so long. There were so many files. Names, dates, account numbers. Her mouth fell open as she accessed document after document.

Classified files.

Diana covered her mouth as she read through profiles on foreign dignitaries and notorious crime lords from around the world. These files contained everything about the person in question, including their family members and their routines. What was all this?

As she kept reading, her stomach seized up. The people in these files were not good men. Certainly not the kind of men she wanted to have information on.

Drug lords, murderers, terrorists and human traffickers. Why would Rafe have profiles on these men? If Rafe associated with these kinds of people, he couldn't be the man she thought he was.

Then she opened another file, and her father's face filled the screen.

Her head spun.

Diana gasped so loudly she wouldn't have been surprised if it woke Rafe, but she was too riveted to even notice. She stared back into her father's eyes, confronted with the face she hadn't seen in so long. Tears filled her eyes as that awful night came back.

It was one thing to think that Rafe had information about her father's death, but this was too much, seeing the evidence that he'd studied her father, looked for an opportunity to hurt him. A choked whimper escaped her lips, and she was on the verge of closing the file when something stopped her. She'd come this far and wouldn't back down now. It was time to find out exactly why Rafe had done this. What had he wanted? Was it politically motivated, or had her father just pissed off the wrong person and paid the price with his life?

Diana took a deep breath and forced herself to start reading. Just like the others, it detailed all her father's information along with his family at the top. That was the only part that was familiar. As she read, heat flushed her body and her stomach roiled.

What the hell?

Who had written this report? The man they described was not her father. A drug trafficker? Human trafficking? Her stomach protested and bile rose in her throat. Diana clapped a hand over her mouth, afraid she'd vomit right then and there. Her father would have never done those things.

Then she moved to the next page, and her heart sank again as she scrolled through pictures of her father standing with armed men, looking for all the world like he belonged there. Then there was a picture of him with Uncle Boris, and the notation next to his name indicated that he was also a wanted criminal in several countries.

That was when Diana realized that *nothing* was as it seemed.

Diana closed her eyes. Of course. How naïve she'd been. Her father was one of these men. The men whom people feared.

One line on the page had her frowning. It was the

report of an exchange of funds from Boris Klinkov to her father. *You don't have time to go down this rabbit hole.* But she couldn't help herself. She clicked the file name.

Boris Klinkov was a family friend. She'd grown up calling him Uncle Boris. He was involved in these horrible things too? Was anyone who she thought they were? Had her mother known?

Too sick to keep reading and too afraid to not continue, she scanned the page. Boris Klinkov had given her father twenty million dollars. In exchange, on her twenty-fifth birthday, she would be married to him, giving him the Jewel of the Sea.

She couldn't hold the bile back anymore. She barely made it to the toilet in the hallway bathroom. Even as she emptied the contents of her stomach, her mind reeled. Her father had sold her. To Uncle Boris. The man was older than her father had been.

You can panic later. Time to run.

With shaking fingers, she took out the thumb drive and put it in her pocket. It felt like she was underwater or moving in slow motion. No matter how hard she tried, she couldn't seem to get her legs to go any faster. All she could see were the horrible things written in that report, and a million questions would start swirling in her brain. Images and memories kept coming back, things that hadn't made sense before but suddenly had whole new meaning in this context.

Suddenly she felt like she had a target on her back. She shivered at the thought of being at the mercy of men like her father. Rafe wouldn't be able to protect her from someone like Boris. From what she'd seen of him and on the files, he was no longer an assassin.

You can't wait for someone to protect you, you need to protect yourself.

This whole time she'd assumed Rafe's past was the obstacle, but she was the one related to criminals. And she'd brought them right to his doorstep. All the contacts she'd used to get her ready for this mission—her brothers' contacts. Criminals. Maybe Uncle Boris had even helped. After all, she was soon to be his property.

Diana closed the computer, stowing it in the duffel. Once it was securely zipped, she slung it over her shoulder. Pausing in the doorway to his bedroom, she took one last look at Rafe sleeping on the bed. Her eyes took in his dark hair falling over his brow and the muscular body that was everything dreams were made of. She stared without blinking, hoping to commit the sight to memory, to burn it into her mind so surely that she'd never forget what almost was.

She needed that memory to get her through what was to come.

CHIRP. *Chirp. Chirp.*

Rafe rolled over and tried to hit the annoying bird outside his window. It didn't stop singing but instead just hopped over to the next windowsill. Frustrated, he tried to reach for it again but couldn't move his arm. Panic filtered through the soft veil of comfort that he'd been wrapped in and he thrashed, trying to free himself. All he accomplished was rolling over and hitting the ground. Hard.

"Ooomph" was about all he could get out before his head started pounding.

Rafe opened one eye carefully and peered around. The room didn't look familiar at first until he saw the legs of his dresser across the room. Why was he looking at the legs? He groaned and managed to turn over onto his back, and when the ceiling came into view, that gave him some answers. The room looked unfamiliar because he'd never seen it from the floor before.

Everything hurt, but Rafe kept his lips clamped together. His limbs were still unresponsive, so his best bet was to remain silent until whatever chemical agent that had been used on him wore off. He would examine things more carefully later to figure out how one of his enemies had managed to get so close. Transitioning into a civilian life made men go soft, but he'd been so sure that his security was tight. The idea that someone could actually get close enough to drug him was maddening. Then he remembered that he hadn't been alone before he fell asleep, and his heart leaped.

Diana. What had they done to Diana?

Strength he didn't know he had roared through his veins, and he managed to roll over and push up onto his arms. His head swam in a sickening wave, and he panted through his mouth, helpless, battling back dizziness and nausea. He had to fight through. He had to make sure she was safe. But once he was able to move again, he had to concede that he wouldn't be much help to her as weak as he was, if she was even still there. Nevertheless, he pushed to his knees. It took quite a bit of effort, but he managed to stumble down the hall. Diana's room was empty. He kept going to his office.

As soon as he walked in, his eyes went to the painting. The safe was wide open.

God. If they'd taken what was in the safe, then there was no doubt this was an ORUS job. Who the hell else would even care about the files he'd kept or go through the extreme security measures to access them? It also meant that Diana was likely already dead. A dull moan slipped from his lips as he struggled to remain upright.

Diana, his poor, sweet Diana, wouldn't have stood a chance against an ORUS-trained hit man. Despair unlike anything he'd ever known swept through him.

He had to call Noah and Lucia. He had to warn them. Maybe they could find out who'd done this. Rafe needed to know. If it took him the rest of his life, he'd find out who'd hurt Diana and make them pay.

Then he remembered his cameras.

Anyone ORUS deemed capable of taking him on would have disabled most of the cameras, but with his training, he knew how to hide a few that might not have been found. His laptop was still on his desk, so he dragged himself over to it and used his fingerprint to boot it up. When he opened the security system and saw that it hadn't been disabled or tampered with, he faltered. What the hell?

Even with a new Orion in charge, there was no way an ORUS agent would be this sloppy. For the first time, Rafe looked down at himself and forced the fog to clear from his mind. Nothing about this made sense. He'd been in the bed, vulnerable and unable to defend himself. So why was he still alive? What kind of job was this where they'd open his safe and take Diana but wouldn't kill him?

He pulled up the video for the day and sped through until the timestamp showed a few hours ago. Then he saw Diana walk out of the front door with a duffel over her shoulder. Alone.

Rafe rewound the video and watched it again, searching her face for signs of coercion. Was there someone else who'd threatened her and made her leave? There didn't appear to be anyone else in the video. Why would she just leave in the middle of the night?

Then he thought about the way he'd woken up, obviously after being drugged, and he looked back at the video. He paused it on Diana's face.

"Who the hell are you?"

THANK YOU for reading the first book of the DEEP duet. The next book, *Deeper*, releases on 1/29/18. PREORDER NOW at malonesquared.com/deeper

While you're waiting, catch up on Jonas and JJ's hilarious antics in their steamy, suspenseful novel - ***FORCE***.

EXCERPT OF FORCE © AUGUST 2017 M. MALONE AND NANA MALONE

JESSICA JONES CLOSED HER EYES, exhausted. Day after draining day of pulling double duty while her bestie and partner in crime was on maternity leave was starting to take its toll. Like hell was she going to start complaining, though. If anyone deserved happiness, it was Lucia. Her best friend had been to hell and back and deserved the time off.

JJ could deal. After all Lucia would do it for her. Besides, JJ wasn't letting a prima donna fashion designer run her into the ground and call uncle. She'd rather burn her Jimmy Choos first. She could handle anything their boss Adriana could dish out.

It felt like she'd only shut her eyes for mere seconds before she frowned in her sleep.

Something was wrong. *Very* wrong.

When she peeled her eyes open again, she was in hell.

"Oh my god," she screamed.

But that scream was her first mistake. It meant emptying out her lungs, which meant she needed to breathe... and that meant lungs full of smoke.

It was so hot her hair plastered against her head and her sheets clung to her naked breasts from sweat. Yeah, she slept topless, so what? It had been so hot lately.

Frantic, she looked around the room trying to find the source of heat. It was so dark she couldn't see anything. But she could feel the smoke all around her, cloying and thick, wrapping around her and constricting her lungs.

"Don't panic." The sound of her own voice out loud scared her out of her frozen state. *Fear immobilizes. Anger motivates.* That's right, get pissed off!

If there was anything JJ was good at, it was being hot

tempered. What the fuck was smoke doing in her room anyway? She'd just had a goddamned blowout. She needed to charge that color and cut to whatever or whoever was the source of this fire.

Move your ass girly.

She had to move because she was *not* dying in this room. She did not survive her past to die like this. Fuck that noise. Besides, if she died like this, Lucia would resurrect her ass and kill her all over again. After Lucia had survived being stalked and almost killed, JJ had a new appreciation for the meaning of life.

She swung her legs over the side of the bed, letting out a sigh of relief when her toes met the carpet. Now that her eyes had adjusted to the dark somewhat, she could see the faint hint of an orange glow from down the hall. Which meant the fire hadn't reached her room... yet.

But the bedroom door stood open to the hall, which was probably why she could already smell the smoke.

It was weird that the door was open. She always closed the door before going to sleep. It was one of the things Lucia's husband had drilled into her. Noah owned a security company, and his overprotectiveness toward Lucia had spilled over onto JJ. Now she always had one of the annoying, albeit sexy, guys who worked for him trailing her to and from work, and her apartment had been subjected to a thorough security 'review' by Noah's resident IT wizard. Matthias had deemed her place 'merely acceptable.'

JJ was pretty sure they'd have asked her to move if they hadn't known from experience that she didn't take suggestions well. The last thing she needed was some man trying to tell her what to do. Maybe Lucia was okay with that, but she wasn't interested. JJ knew from experience that she didn't want any man having control over her life. Never again. That alpha-asshole shit didn't work for her, so they could shove their over protectiveness where the sun didn't shine.

With a quick glance at the open door, she realized it was actually lucky she'd left it open, otherwise she might not have woken up until the flames were closer. What the hell had woken her? *You can think through that shit after you're safe*. Yeah, good point. She grabbed up her comforter and wrapped herself in the thick fabric, bringing it up over her head as she stepped into a pair of slippers.

How far to the door? The window might be an option if the fire escape hadn't been welded over some years ago. She looked up and then squinted in the darkness. And then she saw the shadow in the hall. The man-sized shadow.

Fuck me. She opened her mouth to scream then

reached into her bedside drawer for the nearest weapon she could find. She'd been aiming for the retractable baton she kept in the top drawer. But instead she'd come up with a gag gift from a bachelorette party a couple of years ago. A giant purple vibrator.

What are you gonna do with that? Fuck him to death? Well that was a thought.

"Who the hell are you? And what the fuck are you doing in my apartment?"

He stepped forward slightly, his body still half-hidden outside the door, and JJ raised her makeshift weapon.

"I'm here for you, Jessica. I'm always here for you."

JJ clutched the blanket closer, and her fingers curled around the vibrator as his voice washed over her. The low tone of his words sliced through her veins. That voice. It had been so long since she'd heard that voice. She'd hoped to never hear it again, except in her nightmares.

"How did you find me?"

His chuckle was almost as terrifying as the words that followed. "I never lost you."

JJ screamed and backed up so fast that she stumbled and fell on the bed. The comforter tangled around her and she fought against it, certain the next touch she'd feel would be the last.

Strong hands wrapped around her flailing arms.

"Damn it, you crazy woman, I'm trying to help you!"

It took a few seconds before she recognized the voice, her terror distorting it into the one she feared most. When she finally spoke, her voice was tiny.

"Jonas? Is that you?"

The comforter was pulled back away from her eyes, and Jonas's handsome face appeared. Jonas Castillo worked for Noah's security company and was a regular fixture in her life. He was routinely assigned to protect Lucia, and by default JJ, during the workweek. She took great pleasure in giving him hell, and he was usually cursing her name or bickering with her.

"Yes, of course it's me."

Before she could question what he was doing there, she felt herself being lifted. She clutched his shoulders automatically, disoriented after her fall. Now she wasn't sure if that had actually happened. Had she been dreaming? It was so hard to tell.

"Jonas, did you see anyone else in the apartment?"

"Like who? Don't you live alone?"

Was that jealousy in his voice? Even under these circumstances, JJ couldn't resist the urge to screw with him a little.

"Actually I don't. We can't leave without my favorite guy."

"Who? And if you have a boyfriend, where is he? Some help he is during an emergency."

"Well, Fluffy has never been much help during emergencies, but he blows the best wet kisses."

Jonas didn't pause. "I'll come back for your dog, I promise. But I have to get you to safety."

It must have been the smoke affecting her brain, because at first JJ didn't realize what he'd said. It wasn't until they were at the front door that she understood he meant to leave.

"No! I have to get Fluffy!" JJ swatted at his massive chest. She must have surprised him because his arms loosened around her legs, giving her the room she needed to jump down.

"Damn it, JJ! This is serious. We don't have time to stop."

"It'll just take a second." JJ raced back to the guest bedroom and grabbed Fluffy, covering him with the comforter as she ran.

Jonas picked her up as soon as she hit the hallway and ran for the front door. They passed a crew of firefighters in the corridor outside her apartment. The smoke was thicker out here, so JJ buried her face in Jonas's shoulder, making sure to keep Fluffy covered too.

When they got outside, Jonas set them down carefully on the grass, safely away from the building. An

EMT approached, and Jonas pointed at JJ. She was going to protest, but dissolved into a coughing fit as soon as she opened her mouth. The young man frowned and knelt on the grass next to her. Then his eyes widened when her comforter slipped and she almost flashed an entire boob at him.

"Hey, eyes up, kid." Jonas glared at him before yanking his shirt off. He put it over JJ's head, and she maneuvered carefully to get her arms in without dropping the comforter completely. If she hadn't felt so crappy, she'd have told him exactly where he could shove it. She didn't need anyone speaking for her.

Just to annoy him, she gave the EMT a bright smile that had the young man blushing furiously. Jonas scowled at both of them.

After a flurry of activity, blood pressure cuffs, and oxygen, they finally left her alone. That's when Jonas got a good look at her again. Her *and* Fluffy.

"A fish? You risked your life to save a fucking fish?"

JJ scooped up Fluffy's bowl protectively. "Fluffy is not just a fish. He's a Japanese fighting fish. A total badass."

Jonas looked like he wanted to strangle her. Normally that was exactly the effect she was going for, but strangely, it wasn't as satisfying as usual.

"Thank you, Jonas. For coming in after me."

He looked as shocked as she felt by her sudden gratitude.

"Of course. It's nothing. The fire department would have gotten to you soon. I just happened to get there first when Matthias said your alarms were triggered."

The talk of alarms brought back memories of the man she'd seen in the smoke. It had happened so fast, and she couldn't be sure what was real and what had been a dream.

"Did you see anyone in there?" At his confused look, JJ clarified, "In my apartment?"

Jonas knelt and looked her in the eye. "Was there someone in there with you, Jessica?"

It was all such a blur, and she didn't like the way he was looking at her. Noah's entire crew was extremely overprotective, so if she said the wrong thing, she'd end up on house arrest with Jonas as her jailor. Plus, it was likely it had all been a dream. Jonas had been in her apartment. He would have seen if anyone else was there. The man in the smoke was nothing more than a shadow from a past she'd rather forget.

"No, I meant in the building. I just want to make sure all my neighbors got out okay."

Jonas looked like he wanted to say something else, but Noah arrived just then with Lucia right behind him.

JJ accepted a hug from her friend, and that was when it really hit her.

"I guess I'm homeless now."

Noah's voice carried from behind Lucia. "You'll stay with us, of course."

JJ's eyes met Jonas's, and she knew he was thinking about her earlier question.

"It's for the best," Jonas said.

She glanced over at Lucia. "Free rent and a house full of hot men. Count me in."

* * Get **FORCE** now at www.malonesquared.com/force

ABOUT THE AUTHORS

NYT & USA Today Bestselling author **M. MALONE** lives in the Washington, D.C. metro area with her three favorite guys: her husband and their two sons. She holds a Master's degree in Business from a prestigious college that would no doubt be scandalized at how she's using her expensive education.

Independently published, she has sold more than 1/2 million ebooks in her two series THE ALEXANDERS and BLUE-COLLAR BILLIONAIRES. Since starting her indie journey in 2011 with the runaway bestselling novella "Teasing Trent", her work has appeared on the New York Times and USA Today bestseller lists more than a dozen times. She's now a full-time writer and spends 99.8% of her time in her pajamas. **minx-malone.com**

USA Today Bestselling Author, **NANA MALONE**'s love of all things romance and adventure started with a tattered romantic suspense she borrowed from her cousin on a sultry summer afternoon in Ghana at a precocious thirteen. She's been in love with kick butt heroines ever since.

With her overactive imagination, and channeling her inner Buffy, it was only a matter a time before she started creating her own characters. Waiting for her chance at a job as a ninja assassin, Nana, meantime works out her drama, passion and sass with fictional characters every bit as sassy and kick butt as she thinks she is. **nanamaloneromance.net**

CPSIA information can be obtained
at www.ICGtesting.com
Printed in the USA
LVOW12s1716250118
563853LV00024B/30/P